# Building You Up

## THE NOVEL & SOUNDTRACK

BY ALEXANDRA ALLER

For Amanda, Danielle, Giulianna, Giovanna, and Jason.

# Table of Contents

(*) listen to corresponding track

"It made me think that everything was about to arrive.
The moment when you know all and everything is
decided forever."

- Jack Kerouac

# TABLE OF CONTENTS

# 1

# Weather Woman *

When I was little, the weather woman on the TV said to, "go where the skies are pretty." It sounded like a song to me then. Now I hear the words loop in my head on the days I can't bear to look towards it. To crane the neck, to lift sunken shutters, sometimes feels to me, the most cumbersome and unfathomably impossible chore. Even in skyscrapers, standing on the two-hundredth floor firmly planted atop steel beams and impossible feats of architecture, my first instinct is to look down.

The second hand of the clock dropped. It did not tick. It rang mechanical bursts through the Advisement Center. My lashes kissed at the root, damp from the warm mucous at my water line and I imagined each weightless step out of the building for the very last time. What does the air taste like when your entire life is about to change?

"Miss Ciel."

I sat across from my academic advisor and English teacher, Mr. Salem for a final meeting before transferring to a new school in September for my Senior year. Though he always had the same disappointment carved into his brow, he seemed nervous for me now. But it didn't make a difference if the window I would stare out of during class was here or on the other side of the planet. It would still just be a window.

*What does the air taste like when your*

*entire life is about to change?*

I thought maybe I would miss the sight or smell. Then my cavities filled with the fragrance of cellophane bundled orchids, blown in from the graveyard through the cracked open frame. A high school propped against a cemetery. It's almost too ironic to be true, but it is. Our starry eyes wandered up the cobblestone roads that waned into an actual valley of death's horizon. The school sank an inch every year, just like all of those dead bodies in the ground.

"Miss Ciel." The words spat out from beneath his grey mustache, catching on the rotting weeds of his mouth.

*I can hear you.*

"Well I can see you're not too worried about it. Luckily, community colleges will basically accept anyone if you choose to go down that road, if ever that is. I would strongly advise you to look into them. We should be all set here." He pursed his chapped lips.

Despite Mr. Salem's best efforts to elicit an emotional reaction, I would not grant him the satisfaction. He said, "anyone," like a sharp plastic capped thumbtack into my skin. Of course, it made me angry, to have him sit there, staring at me like the gunk stuck to the bottom of his nautical loafers. *You don't even own a fucking boat.* It infuriated me that a person in a position of authority meant to guide the youth could be so dense. To think that my cold demeanor was just laziness, when it was really a remarkable practice of human restraint. It had taken every ounce of willpower not to burst from the seams, as a warm rage rose up from my uncomfortably juvenile core. I wanted to scream at his big ugly head and call out his life's work as an egregious act of terror on the students of East Queens High School. Instead, I swiped my file from his greasy fingers and stood to leave his office. But not before looking over my shoulder one last time to inform him, "You're a prick."

Looking back on my junior year is like walking through fog. Some things I remember clearly but most of it is just fuzzy. How much of it do they really expect us to remember anyway? Sitting through last period, the doodles on the corner of my desk would shift and grow into a vacuous black hole. I might slip and fall forever. And then the bell would ring. There was always tomorrow.

Though I can remember the feeling of breaking my leg when I was ten and the unrest of bones that didn't fit into skin – I know it was less painful than trying to fit into huddled masses at lunch. Now all of that conditioning was for nothing. I'd have to start over, develop new survival tactics - make new friends I didn't like, figure out which hallways to avoid, suck up to the nurse so she'd let me eat lunch in her office. All the faces I walked past every single day - I already couldn't remember what they looked like.

During Chemistry, I would look out at the droplets of water on the windowpane and think to myself, that I must have been the reason why it rained; that the clouds that felt like bricks in my head, were really up there in the sky.

This one day, the teacher accused us of being too dramatic, too emotional, too soft; on account of all the raging hormones, thunderous pheromones, and the insatiable biology - naturally. So even with the knowledge of such raging, thunderous and insatiable makings inside of our bodies and brains, they still couldn't give us a damn break.

For all their observances of our chemical composure or lack of, they didn't notice the little bit of magic winking out in our eyes. And as that romantic gaze of the world waned so did all my precious lenses crack. Maybe a sheltered youth is an illusion. Maybe none of us ever get enough time.

*And as that romantic gaze of the world waned*

*so did all my precious lenses crack.*

Maybe one day I would look back and I would remember the cemetery, where it began and ended. One day those acres would grow over the plot of land where the youth once learned and danced with such raging, thunderous, insatiable hearts. The double doors did not fly open with triumph, I simply pushed one half open and the air tasted like it always did.

---

I waited on the steps of the school about forty minutes for my mother to pick me up. My mother, who me and my younger brother Kenny, hadn't lived with since we were little kids. Instead, we had lived with our Aunt Nadine who took us in as her own, who would yell at my mother over the phone for letting us eat so much sugar that it gave us stomach aches. But now Aunt Nadine is gone.

"Come on baby, we're tryna' beat traffic!" Mom yelled from the driver's seat.

Chris, my mom's boyfriend, sat in the passenger side asleep. I can't remember a time of her - without him. Kenny was already fast asleep with his face covered by the hood of his sweater.

"You ready?" Mom said excitedly gripping at the worn-down steering wheel, just the two of us awake. The ceiling was littered with cigarette holes and orange foam crumbling down. I half smiled, hugged my bag into my chest and looked back one last time at my old school and the way even the rose bushes looked dreary in that place.

We drove away from a stained apartment in Glendale and towards a sparkling town called Old Westbury in Nassau County. Just under an hour away from the burroughs by car and a world away from crowded blocks of quaint brown bricked homes.

Chris's mother passed away from cirrhosis of the liver and left him his childhood home. In the ten years on the market, Chris had refused every offer from prospective buyers. Taxes on the house were too high to continue paying rent in the city. Chris argued the town was filled with pompous and prying neighbors, but Mom insisted the move would be the fresh start we all needed.

Mom didn't know about Chris' wealthy family when he introduced himself at the Friday meeting at Joan of Arc church. Aunt Nadine said, "it was good luck, not taste." Mom just got her seven-year chip and Chris was working on his collection of day ones. His mother Jean had passed away over a decade ago, but his eyes still watered at any mention of her. He said that she was a saint and the only person who never gave up on him though, "she should have." Saint Jean.

Mom called her a "specific lady." I don't remember much though. I only met her a handful of times when me and Kenny were little. Mom would pick us up for our Sunday breakfasts at Glendale diner where she would let me order whipped cream and chocolate chips on my pancakes. Saint Jean would walk in with big colorful church hats and wiggle into the booth beside me. I didn't like having to sit next to her because she smelled so awful that it made my food taste funny. Now I know she smelled like cigarettes and musky perfume. I remember her tarred fingertips and the way she would crush my cheeks between her palms and bursting pupils  perched on translucent pillows beneath her eyes. "You look just like her," she would coo.

I wore a black dress with pink sneakers to Saint Jean's funeral and I didn't feel sad the way I know I should have. Aunt Nadine held my hand and told me that she was a very sad woman and it's why she drank. "Like mommy? Is mommy sad?" I asked her.

I figured then, that if drinking was the only thing that made Chris' mother happy, then at least she died smiling. After the funeral, I could count on both hands the number of times I saw my mother that year. Maybe Chris needed her more.

I laid my head against the car window with my headphones plugged tightly over my ears. I tried to paint the picture of one of my scribblings. I had been writing myself into metaphors. There was one I really liked, where I was this giant abandoned brick building in the middle of a wide-open field, overgrown with yellow dandelion weeds - which I've always found to be very nice despite people calling them a nuisance. Once scheduled for demolition but now forgotten and protected by the willow trees and vines concealing its appearance. The world had been kind enough not to tear it down entirely, but stern enough to let it build itself back up again on its own. By moving away, I felt that I was somehow losing out on this time I had invested into my construction. I would now be left to a life of cabinets without handles and faucets that only ran piping hot, leaving them simply unbearable to touch. Maybe I'll come back some day and my memory would be kinder to it.

When I opened my eyes, the car slowed to a stop, turning the bend to reveal a red brick, blue shuttered house in dire need of its own repairs. It was modest compared to the other homes around, but just like the rest of them, it looked plastic and flimsy, two dimensional, drawn up, the opening of a laugh track sitcom. Looking up at the baby blue colored-in sky, nothing felt different, not even on what appeared to be the other side of living.

The key snapped out from the ignition. Kenny untangled himself from his headphone wires and sweater strings, groaning and stretching his arms. Chris twisted back towards us, pushing his wire framed glasses up the hill of his straight nose and said with a big cheesy smile plastered from cheek to cheek, "You guys ready?"

He didn't need glasses, they were nonprescription.

## 2

# Ben's Eagle

Seventeen hours had passed since we arrived the prior day's afternoon. Out of those seventeen hours, I slept for ten of them, didn't speak for forty-five minutes straight, felt the saliva cement my cheeks to my teeth bones, ingested food for thirty-four minutes, listened to music and stared at the sky for two hours off the end of the diving board hovering over infected chlorine water, spent twenty six minutes under hot water in the shower, twenty nine minutes sitting in the empty tub with my knees pulled into my chest and the remaining three hours and five minutes dodging my mother bossing around the movers and sitting on the front steps with Kenny hoping that someone would walk by.

No one did. It was just really hot, and I think my scalp got sunburnt. Press repeat.

Another morning played like a sad song, inching towards the dawn. The house buzzed; the sun crawled on its knees through the rattling window frames. The smell of stale cigarettes and black coffee came steaming up from the apricot carpet and into the thick summer air. I rose from the naked mattress on the floor and felt the morning rush of blood plummet down my veins. I often wondered if everyone had felt their blood struggling through the capillaries or if it was just low iron like the school nurses had told me.

Kenny crinkled beneath a thin white sheet, his dark hair in every direction. "Where you going?" He said, rusty like the sun had gotten into him.

"Coffee." I would make coffee, I would spend three minutes making the coffee and an hour sipping the coffee very, very slowly.

I walked down the quiet hall lined with fading wallpaper and sun bleached burgundy carpet, the balls of my feet pressing against short scratchy strands. My steps felt heavy against the hollow ground, like I could shoot through the layers of floor and plaster. The planks of wood would lock me by the calves, so deep in, the wood thought it was back on its weeping willow trunk and begin wildly springing roots through my limbs, fusing with my veins. Within minutes the entire house's electric wiring would be dependent on my REM sleep cycles. There was this weird quirk where every time my eye twitched, the blender would just go off. Naturally they tried to get rid of the blender first because it was a serious safety hazard, but there was simply no getting rid of the appliances. The plugs weren't just jammed in the outlets, they were locked. Forget about cutting the chords, they grew back at the speed of light and sparked so thunderously that anyone within five feet of its split coils were a goner. They begged and pleaded with me to let go, to let go of the house, but they didn't understand that it wasn't my choice to be knee deep in the foundation. At first, it was a clumsy trip but now... but now the house needed me. I wasn't the reason - I was the reaction of all time's doings. And I was fast as fast, fast like fire, could clog like smoke.

I couldn't leave it there to die, its windows blackened, it's light fixtures without their buzzing moths, its door's knobs without hands to hold, its drains starved of rivers. I wasn't just stuck in it. It had become a part of who I was. So they left me there in the hallway with a lampshade over my head and told their guests I was an oddly placed piece of furniture the architects had their reasons for; the way people say everything happens for a reason when they don't want to tell you the truth. They don't know what the hell they're doing either.

But I did not shoot through the ground and spring from the roots. Not this time. I walked over it the way people pulled by gravity do. As of sixteen hours ago, my favorite room in the house was the "sunroom." As of fifteen hours and forty- three minutes ago, I can tell you that a sunroom is a room inside of a large home that simply has a lot of big windows so the light pours in. Hence - sunroom. This was thoroughly explained to me by Chris who likes to make conversation by giving lengthy explanations to very simple concepts that could have been otherwise assumed by a person who spoke relatively good English.

I stood before the room's entrance, framed by two beautiful giant French doors. And though they had been jiggled free from their joints countless times in the days passed, each time you touched the door handles, they seemed to shake free from an eternity of grime and rust. I guess, we're all trying to shake the dead skin off for forever. At the other end of the room were windows that reached from floor to the yellowed tipsy topsy ceiling. The room felt wider than the whole house's frame but so quaint that I imagined it to be the home of a person who lived in the crack of a mountain. Tweed coffee colored couches with plaid fabric pillows squared off the room, pictures with smiling vintage faces hung on the wall, bronze basketball trophies lined the fireplace mantel, TV dinner tables stood open near the love seat, burnt orange shag carpet covered every inch of the room. I skimmed my fingertips across a shelf, sweeping a layer of fairy dust into the air, watching the little mites ride the gust. The windows looked out into a field beyond the backyards wooden planked fence, with green luscious trees almost swallowing the black telephone wires before it.

The leaves did not sway or dance in the morning wind, they sweltered on their branches in the August heat, praying in stillness. I closed my eyes, looking through the neon white of closed lids, feeling as if I was a part of a memory that did not belong to me and in that memory, the only air left to breathe was an infused hushed jacaranda hue. My lungs filled with the color and I knew that I was not the only person breathing life into the room.

"Oh, hi baby," Mom said from behind me. I jumped at the unfamiliar voice. "Oh, I'm sorry," she laughed. "What are you doing up so early? It's a Saturday. Aren't teenagers supposed to sleep in?"

"I couldn't sleep. It's too hot." I was never a good sleeper or so Aunt Nadine told me.

"Yeah, you did get to bed pretty early last night. We missed you at dinner. Well you know," she groaned, wiping the sweat from her brow, "- we're gonna fix the air conditioning all over this house pronto." Mom's hair was permanently 80's high, emotive, lifting with excitement and flattening out like a scolded dog's ears with shame and sadness. Her black curls seemed to tighten with each word she said now.

"How you feeling?" I asked, hooking my fingers around my wrist.

"Good, good. I'm just fine. Why don't I look ok?"

"Yeah, you look fine," I said.

"Chris said there's a community pool somewhere close by. That'd be a great way to make some new friends," she rushed through her words. The sweat continued to drip softly down her face. Her fingertips trembled, from nerves and an empty gut. I nodded and looked back out towards the yard. "I'm gonna go make some coffee," she said exhaling deeply, seeming frustrated.

Mom wasn't just some addict. She was hurt very badly by life. I hated the idea of what people must have thought about her, but I know she hated it more. She and my father had been seventeen when they decided to run away together after she got pregnant. I used to hang on her every word when she told us stories. I thought every little kid grew up hearing fairy tales like that, but fairytales aren't supposed to end like it actually happened. They were so madly in love that there was no doubt in their minds about keeping me. Two years later, they had Kenny and were working towards their GED's together and a down payment on a home. She said they had friends who came over on Sunday for poker night and picture frames covering every shelf and wall. Mostly everyone left, said I looked like him. I had his brown eyes, his black hair, his smile, his scowl, his caramel skin. I have all these pieces of him locked up inside my DNA and I think it's the reason I'll never be able to shake the feeling that I'm forgetting about something I had to do that was really, really important.

*We're all trying to shake the dead skin off for forever.*

My aunt told me that he was very forgetful too. *Do you see him every time you look at me?* My father died when I was about four-years-old. A drunk truck driver slammed into his car. My mother had nightmares for months about pulling shards of the windshield out of his skin. When she couldn't make the bad dreams stop, she started to drink them away. I try not to blame her, but it's hard when you feel faulted from a pinnacle impact. It's almost easy to not be outwardly angry with her, but bitter doesn't seem to ever really go away, does it? It always serves up a poignant reminder, pumping that fume into your rationale. Sometimes I think about the way my very own eyes weren't ever mine to begin with, just molded to see things this way or that. Like I've got these nuisance glasses sitting at the bridge of my nose and I've just had to see through that lens - just because.

I think you can go a very long time thinking you know someone without ever even touching the surface. That's how I feel about my mother. She doesn't let me see anything because she's scared of what I may think, but what she doesn't know is that she's depriving me of a reason to forgive her. Maybe if I could understand her decisions better, we could be there for one another. I know we both need it. If she would just say sorry, acknowledge the gaping hole in the ground, the orifice spewing sewage into the drinking water, the blazing church on fire - but she'll never be able to. She can't. People need to believe their version of reality to find a way to live with themselves. But the reality is, truth happens differently to each of us.

13

"Coffee!" She screamed from the kitchen. She was trying and it did count for something, but it wasn't enough to barter with yet. The disasters had outweighed the relief. Coffee always does seem to help though.

The smell of coffee in the morning is a part of every New Yorker's liberal rights. Those rights were passed down to me by my mother and her mother before that and her great mother before that and her supreme mother before that. It's a part of the constitution nailed to every bus and subway stop and in very fine print down at the bottom, it says, "Trust me, you're going to need this." Growing up in New York is like being in on the joke. You're never alone when you're in on it. Side streets are for natives, main roads are for transplants. Bodegas are for city kids and corporation cafes are for bridge and tunnel kids. Cops - bad. Firefighters - good. Don't talk to crazy people, give your seat up for pregnant ladies, don't get your ass kicked, be nice to your butcher and no matter what, do not touch the railing on the subway stairs. Every inch of New York has been pissed on, puked over and shit on, and yet it's still the city where people go to dig up their dreams from out of their pockets filled with pennies and cigarette buds. Growing up in New York means spending half your time on trains and drinking dollar cups of coffee. There's no such thing as slowing down. There's only getting there. You spend that decade or two or five on the express lines and you realize, for someone always in motion you haven't gotten very far.

I'm not sure the trains have anything to do with it. I pieced together all the commandment like statements above, that had been said by Aunt Nadine while either walking through a sardined bus or sitting on a train that passed its stop due to construction.

Aunt Nadine was a true and through cement kid. She called Kenny and I, "the roses that grew from the cracks of the concrete, like the Beats in Time Square. Except you're Nuyorican." That means a New Yorker with Puerto Rican heritage. But the only thing Puerto Rican about us was her cooking. Aunt Nadine would never recite another unspoken law or cook another caldero of yellow rice and beans. What did that make me now? Maybe I would spend forever trying to understand where I came from without ever really belonging to one place.

*... for someone always in motion*

*you haven't gotten very far.*

My thoughts; coffee in the suburbs tastes like lonely and waiting in line at the Post Office. Not my best metaphor. Still true.

We sat around the kitchen table with a pot as our idolatry, the sliced egg bread as a morning treaty. Next to Kenny, Chris seemed frail, with his tattered forearms and scratchy red elbows stabbing onto the table like little daggers.

Kenny sat statuesquely, the way he mostly was, towering over us all, maybe a bit above it too. He said everything was fine, but he had left a boyfriend back in Queens and I know he missed him. Though he didn't talk about the pains he held, they were etched out clearly in his jaw. Discomfort.

"Ok so," Chris murmured awkwardly, "- your rooms are upstairs on the right if you wanna haul up those mattresses from the dining room." He looped his arm around mom and his thick black glasses drooped down to his nostrils. We already knew he switched to sunglasses inside because of his perpetual hangover. The sunlight gave him terrible migraines, but he always insisted on telling child-like fables about him being a vampire and the dawn weakening his strength. I'm still not sure if he even knew how old we actually were or if he just never learned to communicate what he was feeling.

My task for the day was to organize a single bedroom. "Well this is cute, huh?" Mom said passing by with her arms wrapped around a basket of clean laundry. The walls were painted periwinkle with yellowed molding trim running through its center. The floor was checkerboard tiling like you see in corny 50's concept diners. Sticky, too. Next to the skylight, chunky, gaudy teardrop prisms hung like a chandelier from the ceiling fan, except they were tied to its wings with shoelaces. Sparkling little rainbow freckles spattered onto the saran wrapped furniture like Christmas wrapping paper. Cardboard boxes lined the sides of the room like bricks on a wall. I sat on my naked mattress, seemingly out of place here, overwhelmed with the space and sunlight. The room felt too bright to think.

I never thought I would miss Glendale. It never seemed like a place, more like a station. I thought we would make it all out together. I liked purple too, but Aunt Nadine preferred richer tones. We lived right over a laundromat, so it always smelled like dryer sheets. Our bedroom was carpeted with this itchy plum colored rug that left little purple pills on all of my clothing. And there was this skylight in the center of the room that popped out into a small pyramid on the roof and the glass was covered in a thick soot that stayed all throughout the years. The only window in the room opened up to the side of another building's brick wall, but I never minded it much. It was sort of poetic, the way you could fit a handball in there, but nothing wider. I tried to use some chalk to decorate the window, but instead I covered it with curtains and never really went by it again.

I looked out of my new bedroom window to see a run-down powder blue 1960's Cadillac in the driveway of the house across the street. A boy walked out from the front door with his arms loaded with trash bags. The screen door slammed shut behind him. He pulled keys out of his pocket, shimmying one loose into the trunk's lock. It flew open, almost swiping him. He laughed which was strange, I thought, because he almost knocked himself clean. After loading the bags into the car, he leaned against it and with a swift movement, pulled out a cigarette from behind his ear and a lighter from his jean pocket. The nicotine stick was wedged between his lips while he attempted to light the end with one hand and the other cupped around the flame. He closed his eyes and the smoke leaked out from his mouth, into the air above him. A gust of summer wind blew the leaves dangling from branches down onto his shoulders. For a second, I felt this sadness fill me. I would never know what color his eyes were.

A silver haired man in a wheelchair rolled out of the front door and down the long winding walkway. They didn't look alike. The boy's nose was pointy and thin, and the man's nose was Roman like the textbooks. The boy's arms seemed to be too lanky for his body and the man's arms were larger than the wheels on his chair. He handed the boy his silver keys, nodded and said something which seemed amicable enough, but I couldn't make it out. The boy with no color in his eyes turned around, got into the car and drove off. It was a simple exchange with nothing but faint smiles and few words. It was a chore. As the man watched the boy drive away, his face suddenly turned toward me. He waved with a kind smile and spun back around into the house.

"What are you doing?" Kenny's voice came from behind me. I turned around to look at him, about to tell him of the boy with no pigments left in him. I stopped myself.

"I don't know," I exhaled. "This place is weird."

"Yeah," he brushed his hair back. "It's so quiet. I feel like something is about to pop out at me every time I walk past a doorway."

"How's your room?" I asked.

"Well it's pink which I don't hate, but it makes me wonder why Chris gave me that room."

"Kenny, Chris does not care that you're gay," I huffed.

"Yeah, I know. I would have preferred the room with the skylight. I'll go get the scissors," he groaned.

I grabbed the first box off the stack. As I started to unpack, each item seemed more pointless than the last. There were stuffed animals, glue sticks, pins from the past ten years of our life. Plastic, artificial matter.

Aunt Nadine was a borderline hoarder, justifying her obsession with material objects by developing an incredible mastership of organization. When her husband passed away only twenty years into their marriage, it left her completely devastated and she could never seem to let go of his belongings. She used to say, "All that energy, well it needs to go somewhere, it's just got to." She told us that at first, she thought she would hold a garage sale, but every time she went to, the weather woman said to watch out for thunderstorms. Then she packed all of his things into boxes and asked the church to come by to pick it up for the less fortunate but then she had a revelation that she was simply against everything organized religion stood for and she wouldn't pay them for her soul. So, she saved what was left of him; sweaters, watches, tax returns and with it, a power to keep part of him alive. Maybe she was fearful of losing us because she started to save nearly every school project and tissue that we blew our nose into. Though I always found it silly and I still do, it's only now that I truly can empathize. I don't have much to remember her by, but I think if I did, being surrounded by those things would make it better. Even if it were just for a short moment. How is that some people take up more space when they're gone?

*I would never know what color his eyes were.*

*...the boy with no pigments left in him.*

"I think I'm going to become a minimalist," I said. Suddenly, surrounded by trinkets and cardboard, I decided I would shed my cement suit for an inmost tangerine fleshy layer.

"Where did you learn that word?" Kenny laughed.

"I don't know, I think I read it somewhere." I read it in a book about tidying up that I bought for Aunt Nadine. She didn't get around to it and by that, I mean she shoved it under a stack of alphabetized magazines on her dresser.

"Well if that means we don't have to go through another box of my elementary school book reports then I'm game. Why do we still have all this crap anyways?"

"I don't know. Maybe it seemed important to her at the time. You know, someone had to be saving all this stuff... but I guess it doesn't matter now."

He looked sadly at me and said, "This one is clearly some of my best work. We can save this for when I'm rich and famous." It was a finger painting of the three of us at Rockaway beach and my favorite memory of Aunt Nadine. I was in the fifth grade and when my name sounded through the announcement speakers, I arose from my desk with the pride and triumph of a 9-year old who had just received the Nobel Peace Prize.

"Oh, hi baby," she said waiting outside the school doors. We went to Rockaway Beach for the first day of summer, the way her father had done when she was a little girl. It was too cold to go into the water, but I can remember how good the sun felt on my skin. I gazed at her silver strands of curls blowing gently in the wind, her un-ironed caramel face towards the blue sky, the purest expression of happiness I have to remember her by. We stayed there all day reading on beach towels and snacking on plantain chips. My only regret is not having put my feet into the ocean when she asked me to.

The lyrics that swim through my head seem to come from a titanium announcement speaker that sound through every hall in every building in the world. *I am the Contender for your pain.*

When I found Aunt Nadine on the floor of her bedroom, I didn't understand what had happened. But the feeling of her cold skin against my fingertips has never left them. The pain was paralyzing. No sound came from my cries. Panicked, I searched for a pulse, not knowing where it should beat from. Her wrists were so heavy. I had never taken a pulse; I couldn't tell if I was doing it right. I wished I had been doing it wrong, but it turns out that not feeling a pulse is an easy thing to do. Nothing else has been easy since. I'm not sure if anyone can see it.

"Pais....Pais..." Kenny shook my shoulders. "You ok?" He said, wide pupils darting from eye to eye. All of the papers I had been holding in my hands, were now suddenly on the floor.

And it happened like that. Every second I was somewhere, I was really, else - adrift in memories that felt so wet you could float atop the surface of them, waft your fingertips through the pages.

Mom called for us.

---

"Whoa."

There was a door in the backyard that blended into the fence. It let out to a massive field of trees and overgrown grass. For what felt like miles, there was nothing but patchy land and kicked through paths to nowhere. We stepped carefully over the dried leaves.

I wondered how it looked in the rain. The four of us walked carefully in silence, only letting out breaths and creeks at our joints. The song of summer filled our ears, the buzz of a season's goodbye filled my lungs. Did the great listeners of the world know that the Sun made a sound? I think they must have. It's this quiet kind of sizzle but more like a whisper, a quiet kind of brass ring or the sound of a finger tracing the rim of a wine glass. Every season has a farewell tune and if you listen closely, you can start to hear the lyrics, less like a verse and more like an apology, less like a lullaby and more like a secret. Winter is very, very sorry for leaving you out in the cold. Autumn is fearless. Spring is quite tender, never being able to let their lovers go. Spring can really be a dog's jaw, just holding on and on. Sometimes, I feel like Spring needs to get it together -

"What is this place?" Kenny asked. "Like quarantined land or something?"

"The Sump," Chris replied and pointed towards a cardboard sign tucked and propped up on two barren bushes. The words were written sloppily in black marker, almost like they could have read, "Keep Out." The floor was littered with broken green glass and crushed beer cans. There was an old mattress propped up on the side of a hill with its springs protruding through the diamond laced fabric. It was an island of youth, ripped silk, and wild roots.

"This is where we all used to hang out and get into trouble as kids. This is where all the cool parties are or at least where they used to be." Chris said. "God, we had some fun back here. Oh wait, wait," he said running towards a bush. "Is this? Yep, this is where I lost my virginity!"

"Ok ew," Kenny said.

"They called it the cherry pit, get it?" He laughed.

"Chris, really? Really?" Mom scoffed

# 3

# The Great Contender *

I'm not sure anyone finds me beautiful or if someone needing to find you beautiful actually makes it so. I've heard people say a lot of cliche statements on self-worth and how beauty comes from within and I get it, I know those things are supposed to be more important, but they don't feel important when you don't feel beautiful. And I know it's not supposed to matter but it does.

When I'm riding my bike with the wind in my squinted eyes and sun kissing my hair, I feel beautiful and in control.

So I went for a ride and paid attention to the way my hair wisped past my ears and the sherbet sky dripped down all around me. In the city, riding my bike too fast made me feel like I was a part of a neon river whose waters marbled the path through the concrete but here, here the entire world was still - and I was on fire.

Each house looked like the other, the shutters and doors forming abstract faces, quiet and closed mouthed. The thinning rubber hugged the wheels that flew over fresh silky-smooth tar. I could feel every bump in my gut. Pushing the pedals as hard as I could, ripping my way out of the unfair spacetime continuum and then finally, just as I could feel my skin unstick from the fabric of reality, I realized I went in a giant circle.

23

My new jigsaw family moved from room to room with boxes clenched in their arms. There was the blue Cadillac parked outside my neighbor's house again. And there was the man gazing out of the bay windows in his home. This time he didn't see me looking at him. He just stared off motionlessly into the melting sky. The quietness of the suburbs sounded like an infinite song, like the chimes and whistles of a carousel who only ever knew going in circles.

The gentle breeze danced through the hem of my clothing like a thumb trails against skin and the clean summer air hummed like the brass strings ringing out. I could feel my body sinking into it, starting to slip, letting myself feel safe and it struck me like ice. I felt guilty for feeling safe.

"Hey." A voice sang from behind me.

It was the boy once wrung dry of pigments, whose cheeks were now flushed with roses and freckles, whose head sprouted copper curly tendrils and - green eyes. He had green eyes. "You just move in?"

The same winds pushed at his frame. It's so funny to think how we're all taking in the same air and yet it turns us all into such wildly different creatures. The left side of his thin lips curled up like a strand of hair snapping. He wore a yellow t-shirt with the sleeves cuffed and red waxed lettering that read, *Ben's Eagle.*

"Yeah, yesterday," I answered shyly. "Do you live there?" I pointed towards the house across the street.

"Who, with Hank? Nah, he's my Dad's friend. I just help him out sometimes," he shrugged. "I'm on the other side of The Sump.

What about you, where are you folks from?" He asked. *Who says folks?*

"Queens," I said. I could feel my left thumb start to tick in towards my palm. It happened whenever I was nervous, like tearing the sticker off of a glass bottle.

"Oh yeah, yeah. When I was little, we used to go to my grandparents' house in Forest Hills for Hanukkah. Stopped going when they both died so, you know."

"Yeah I get that. It's a nice area though," I offered weakly.

"Um, you're going to CLK too, right? The high school. You live in the district."

"Oh yeah. I forgot about that," I said worried.

He laughed like it was a joke. "What grade are you in?"

"Senior," I shrugged. The thought of school, of another tweed counselor's office chair, it made me want to throw up. There's nothing about high school to make metaphors of, you just get through it.

A spit and sparkling Jeep pulled up to the curb. Ray, short for Rachel, I would later learn. His girlfriend. She looked like one of the girls with shiny upbringings and a kitchen doorway scribbled with every inch she grew. Nuclear and laminated. Eyes that had only ever seen blue skies. She was beautiful, the illusion of her anyway.

"Hey," she barely grinned.

"I gotta go," he said apologetically. "Wait what's your name?"

"Paisley."

"I'm Ben." Like his shirt.

As I walked back into the house, I sang to myself, "Ben, Green, Senior. I am the contender, la, la la..."

---

The transparent skylight in my room was so clean, annoyingly unweathered by the world. How was it that out here, everyone and everything seemed to be so untouched by storms? Did it ever rain? Why did the natural disasters pass over this place? Why had every window I ever looked out of been rickety and gooping with hardened tar at the corners, seen through the spaces of bars? This sickeningly perfect window let in a shade of the night that enveloped my skin and everything in its way into a dark indigo pocket. I was stuck in a film composed of pastels when I was drawn in with bold charcoal strokes, stuck in a world of silicon when I was made of rusted metal.

I imagined what Ray was like. I already didn't like her, and I was aggravated with myself for it. But I couldn't help it. I imagined she smelled like one of the perfume kiosks at Queens Center Mall. I pictured myself standing in the center of a crowded hallway and feeling a cold sharp shoulder push into me. A violent floral scent would follow like the whiff of posies that knocked everyone out in The Wizard of Oz. She stretched, towering above me like a giant expensive doll with dirty blonde, straightened, crisp hair flowing behind her like ribbons. My illusion of beauty was cruel. *Rhetorical fantasies.* Self-inflicted, imagined pain. Oh yes, I'm the great contender.

I opened my eyes. The quiet was still playing like the ending grain on a record. Blood moseyed through my limbs. I could hear my heartbeat inside my skull the way you can hear it when you plug your ears with your fingers. Like a wave. It washed in. I leaked at the eyes again, hoping the spill didn't stain the pillowcase.

"Pais?" Kenny's voice came from the other side of the door.

"Come in," I said hushed. The door creaked and he crawled under the comforter.

"You know what's crazy?" He whispered, shuffling and tucking into bed. "That light coming in from the window... it's from the moon. Not like lamp posts and store windows and car lights... it's just, like brighter out here. And so purple at night. Like things have more color here. But less at the same time too."

*Here comes the purple, the color of love...*

"Kenny, I'm scared," my voice cracked. I felt the salt start to burn my eyelids. "I don't know if I can do this. I don't know what's wrong with me." He gripped my hand into his and squeezed tightly. "I know," he replied. "I'm scared too. But it's not bad, it's just changing."

*... once it's been bruised and changed.*

"But what does it feel like inside of you right now? It's all the time for me now. It's like there's something wrong, like I ... must enjoy feeling this way or something because it feels like I'm doing it to myself at this point."

He squeezed my hand tighter. "It's going to be ok. I promise."

I asked again, "Does it feel that way for you Kenny?"

"What way Pais?" He asked softly, tucking himself in.

"Like it's contagious."

"I don't think so."

"Why does it for me then?"

# 4

# Rrrmmcsst

Cement clouds in my head, propped upon rickety rotten planks of wood as sorry excuses for bones. Something wrong. Broken. Every time I moved, I felt it coming loose again, rattling around out of place. It was stuck inside of me, caught in my throat like a wrench gone horizontal down a pipe. Walking, arms swinging, limbs taken over by miniature trapeze artists trying to balance me like saving a giant from tipping over. The townspeople would gather from far and wide to see the circus tent turned into the main attraction. The lions would rest in tall grasses as arms sprung out from the curtains, tearing at its totem like neck for the invisible object it was choking on. "This could take a while," they said to the hippos in their tanks.

I poured black coffee into a red ceramic cup and inhaled the steam hoping its taste would return to normal. It didn't. The mug once hung from the hooks of Aunt Nadine's kitchen. I wondered if it felt out of place harbored in the spacious wooden pantries of the suburbs. Too much room, not enough space to think.

Chris stumbled into the kitchen, tilted his head beneath the copper faucet and let the water run into his mouth as he let out a growl, an ancient tool lodged somewhere in his intestines. Glutton reverberates.

"Oh, hey Pais, morning," he grunted. "Why don't you do me a solid and make me five cups of coffee?"

"On it." He patted my head. For the average ear it was inaudible but for us, it was ritualistic symbiotic language. The way it was until it wasn't. Coexist. Cohabitate. Co-coffee. He crawled back up the stairs and would not likely return until the late afternoon sun rolled down the window frame. Chris' trust fund had afforded him all hours of the day his entire adult life and he wasted them, every single one of them. The man barely left his room.

"What's for breakfast?" Kenny asked, squeezing at my shoulders. It was almost surreal each time I saw Kenny, my innocent baby brother taller than me, this stunning beautiful boy who smiled and had thoughts and goals that grew strong even in unkempt soil. There he was, the only family I would ever have. To have just one person who I knew would always be a part of me, it seemed too good to be true. And each time I saw him I was scared of losing him, because that's all I've ever really learned of love, that you never get to keep it.

"Coffee and... and part-time job applications," I said dropping the newspaper down onto the table.

"What am I supposed to do with that? What, are we suddenly in the 80's?" He scoffed.

"Could be, who knows what year it is?" I said to the camera.

"How about just the coffee?" he said.

"Actually, I don't think you'll need to do that," Mom said, one eye creaked open, hugging her purse in a white t-shirt and boxers. She clawed out two twenty-dollar bills and slapped them on the table.

"What's this?" I said looking down at the cash.

"Well, you know it's for lunch money and stuff," she shrugged. "I'll get some more from the bank today."

"You don't need to do that," Kenny said eying the newspaper.

"No, no this is the way it should be. You guys should be focusing on school and doing kid things like joining sports stuff and the debate team. You'd be so good at that Pais, you're just so smart baby," she said, folding her lips into her mouth, pearly eyed. Kenny and I looked at one another unsure. "Guys, come on this is what mommies are supposed to do for their babies. The house is paid off and well, you know I meant what I said. Things are going to be different this time around. It's going to be better. You just wait and see." She kissed Kenny's forehead. "I'm gonna go wash up and get ready and then go to the store to get some damn curtains for the bedroom before Chris disintegrates from all that sunlight. Who wants to come with?" We were all having trouble adjusting.

Kenny and I both stared at one another, puzzled.

"Oh, come on, what now?" Mom scoffed.

"It's 8 a.m. Stores don't open for another couple of hours," I offered empathetically.

"I know that. I know that," she beamed. "Come on, come on, the day ain't gonna wait too long," she sang.

31

Kenny rolled his eyes and grabbed the coffee pot from the still air. Who knew it had been hovering in space the whole while?

"She's trying," I said hands numb. "That's worth something."

"Yeah, and I'm not buying."

*... that's all I've ever really learned of love, that you never get to keep it.*

---

"Damn," Mom said, brushing her wild curls back from her forehead. "Where the hell is this place?" She mumbled through the cigarette wedged between her lips. "What the hell is this? Haven't these people ever heard of a grid system? How are you supposed to get on the other damn side of the road? This is just, this is insane. Yeah screw you too buddy!" She screamed through the windshield at a passerby waving his hands angrily at us.

"It's right over there."

"Where?" She said, looking out from under her sunglasses.

"There. Where the woman in a scooter is going into," I said.

"Huh, doesn't she kinda look like grandma?" Mom asked, pulling into the parking lot.

"I mean... if you mean in the way that every older woman in a scooter kinda looks like your mother then yeah... I guess I kinda see it."

---

Her name was Yvie. Pronounced like *Eve-eee*.

She had lime green chopsticks in her hair, a dozen or so rhinestone bracelets down both wrists and matching Chinese slippers from the 99 cent stores on every block in Elmhurst, Queens. The first thing you see when you walk into Lohanne's Fabric is her. I recognized the song buzzing down from the ceiling.

"Hi miss!" Mom waved like a child in class. "Could I..." She peered down at her name tag."-ask you a question Yvie?" Mom butchered the name. Deep crow's feet and soft violet circles scratched out the shape of her round brown eyes. Her hands were fragile, worn in like she had been working her entire life.

"You said it wrong, it's Eve-eee," I corrected her. I recognized the name from a book I read last year in English class. Yvie smiled warmly at me.

"Oh, I'm sorry. Yvie, I'm looking for fabric to make curtains out of."

"You gonna wanna go to aisle five all the way in the back of the store," she said. I couldn't make out her accent.

"Oh, thank you," Mom beamed. "But see the problem is, well I don't know how to make curtains or, well you know sew," she nervously hacked. "I was wondering, do you or someone in the store know how to do that sort of thing?"

"You gonna wanna go to aisle five all the way in the back of the store, pick the fabric you wanna get, take it to the cutting counter and then you gonna wanna go to the sewing center. They show you what you needa' do there."

"Aisle five, you got it," Mom said pointing finger guns. Yvie smiled back politely.

The fluorescent lights above me started to hum like television static. It was comforting like the sound of a movie left on before bed. It seemed like a good place to work, quiet and well, quiet.

"That your momma?" Yvie asked.

"Um… yeah I'm not really sure why she didn't just buy curtains," I said, almost apologetically.

"She gonna do just that when she see the price tag," she chuckled. "You want gum?"

"Sure," I shrugged. "I'm Paisley." She popped a piece of fruit punch pink gum into my palm as she hummed to the music.

"Hey, do you like this song?" I asked her.

"Yeah, it's bitchin," she smiled and winked at me.

"Yeah, it's so good, right?" I said excitedly.

Then Ben's girlfriend walked past the store-front windows. I almost didn't recognize her with her hair thrown messily into a bun bopping around as she walked, swimming in a massive Harvard sweater. A pale and freckled redhead wearing a purple velour jumpsuit walked beside her. They just laughed back and forth with their jaws dropped so far down you could see the blood stretched out from their lips. Blotched pale skin.

"Hi Yvie!" Rachel said giddy and waving as she pushed the front door open.

"Hello," Yvie said back. Rachel was beautiful. Airy, bright. She seemed happy. "That girl a pain in my ass. Her voice. It never stop," she said beneath her breath. She pulled out a sticker gun and walked out from the counter. "Never stop," she shook her head. "You want another piece of gum?" She asked me again.

"I think I'm good, thanks," I smiled.

"Hey, you looking for a job?"

"Yeah. I am. Yeah, I am looking for one. But I'm in school so I need to figure out the time," I stuttered through, nervously again.

"You come back when you figure it out. You can work here. The girls gonna love you," she smiled warmly. "I see you soon."

"Pais, what are you doing?" Mom said from behind me. "Come help me pick this fabric. I can't decide on anything by myself," she said holding up two shades of Navy, only one slightly darker than the other.

"They look... the same," I lied.

"Ugh you're no help," she stormed off.

I walked through the aisles of fabric rolls on racks, through rows of color coordinated planks of starch cloths, down an aisle dedicated entirely to all the different types of glue in the world, past the wedding aisle with plastic rose petals in sharp cornered boxes impossible to open up with the average pair of scissors and then -

"Ray, Ray, I found them!" I heard a voice shout. I walked closer to the voices until I could hear them from the other side. "Ok I need to find a capital B." Metal nails on chalkboard. "What?" I couldn't tell the difference between the two girls' voices. They sounded creepily identical in high pitch, accent and tone. They spoke exasperatedly and forced a whine into each vowel.

"B for Ben?" The girls laughed. "Kelly, he is just you know... so frikken pretty." They erupted in laughter again. "I can't believe you did that in the sump last night."

"Ok, you did it too, Kelly."

"Oh my god that does not count. We hooked up like a million times before that."

"Ok, you hooked up twice before that and the second time doesn't count cause he was so drunk he was licking the back of your knee."

"Whatever, it was nice. It was like... like sensual, you know?" The girl made the sucking sound of pressing your tongue to the top of your mouth. Tst. "Whatever. I want more deets. Like what does it look like? Oh my God, for Halloween we should just wear like booty shorts, bras and then you wear an "R" and I'll wear "Kelly". We can be R. Kelly. Oh my god, we have to!"

"That's genius. Down." The girls either high five'd or someone slapped the other.

"I wonder if me and Ben are still gonna be dating though like, by then you know? It's only a month away. He can be so weird. I mean I like that, he's like mysterious, but weird. Yesterday I was like come over cause my parents are out and he goes... "I can't, I'm on the last three chapters." Like what does that even mean? And I know he doesn't study. I bet you it was one of those weird Asian porn comics. He's so weird."

"Ew, what a weirdo," the other chronicled.

*The sound of my eyeballs rolling in mucous. Rrrmmcstt.*

"I know, how weird, right? He's such a dork, but like it's cute, you know? He's cute."

"He's cute," I mimicked silently with my face scrunched up.

"Oh my God, that's literally amazing. You and Ben. Like who would have seen it coming? I didn't see it coming, like at all." God, it was so frustrating to listen to them speak and gasp, then speak and squeal and repeat. It was like they wanted to be heard just so they could torture the unfortunate ears in close enough proximity. Did they realize they were speaking out loud?

"What are you doing?" Mom said from behind me.

I leapt up in a panic, knocking my head into the corner of the metal shelf and the row of paint bottles from it. I heard one of the girls say, "what was that?"

Yvie stood there with her sticker gun, blowing a bubble. Mom clenched the two fabric rolls in her arms. I tried to cup the fast-growing bump on my head with my hand but recoiled on contact. My face shrunk in embarrassment. I spat out, "I dropped a contact."

"You don't wear contacts," Mom said confused. "Wait, do you?

# 5

# I like your wrists *

Aunt Nadine used to say I was special because I was the kind of person meant for just a few and not many. It sounded like a compliment at the time, but now it feels like some kind of spell she accidentally cast. But not Kenny. Kenny had tons of friends, was always great at sports and did good in school. On his first day of high school, he sat next to me in the cafeteria and then one day there were so many people squeezing onto the bench, I had to find somewhere else to sit. I know it might sound like I'm jealous and that's because I used to be. Now, I don't envy his capacity for socializing or surpassing academic *and* athletic expectations. It seems tedious. I find existing difficult enough already without even thinking about how to change or improve it.

I tagged along to Kenny's first baseball practice and parked on to the metallic bleachers, still wet from the morning rain. A musk hovered in the grey mist. Small puddles of muddy water tacked along the sides of the field encircled with red clay colored track. Blue skies, sunken ground, surrounded by pastel homes and towering streetlamps.

I felt a tap on my shoulder and rushed to slip my headphones off. "Hey, mind if I sit here?" A girl asked me. She had long black hair and beautiful warm brown eyes.

"Yeah, sure." I smiled politely.

"Cool, I'm Giuls," she said, throwing her bag down. "You're the new girl, right?"

"Yeah I guess so," I said, suspiciously.

"Good." She pulled out a cigarette. "You want some?" I shook my head to say no. "So, which one is your boyfriend?"

"No. No, I'm just Kenny's sister." I pointed at him on the field. She was neutral, almost bland. I appreciated how blunt she was though, instead of high beaming me with a smile I felt obligated to return. "Whose yours?"

"Will, number eleven. He's not my boyfriend though. We just, you know, hangout."

The dreadful jumpsuits floated towards us, their ominous velvet catching the lightning like static, riding the thunder in. Their neon eyes sparkled, staring through the chain link fence, their polluting atmospheric laughter roared, and mumbled whispers sounded like the hush in the eye of a storm. "I'm right here Maggie, might be easier for me to hear if you spoke up," Giuls said, bravely.

"Oh, I'm so sorry. I said, you turned into a druggie weirdo ever since you started dating Will. Loud enough for you?" Maggie yapped, with plump glossed lips. I imagined tiny fruit flies stuck in their goop. They walked away in silence. *Bzzz.*

"You ok?" I asked, hesitantly.

"Oh no, I'm good," she chuckled. "I've basically seen her faceplant into snow. She's just mad cause I stopped talking to her this summer... because she's an asshole!" She shouted at them.

"Someone call my name?" It was Ben. Senior. Green eyes. He sat down next to me, lifting his muddied sneakers onto to the bleacher steps. There was a cigarette behind his ear, one of his curls wrapping around it.

"Wow who knew it was a conch call?" Giuls laughed. "This is the new girl... what's your name again?" She asked.

"Paisley," Ben answered, smiling at me. I felt my cheeks rush with blood. I turned my face trying to hide them. He snickered. He looked the way a match being struck sounds, a blow-dryer snapping up into high, the first strum of a freshly tuned guitar, blinds dropping to the bottom of a windowsill, the gush of water through pipes before a shower - "Yeah, I know."

"Should have known you already got to her," Giuls said, blowing out smoke. It was weed, not tobacco.

"What is that supposed to mean?" Ben laughed. "You're making me sound like a creep."

"You are a creep," Giuls said, somewhat playfully.

"I'm not a creep. I promise," he said to me. He was wearing the same yellow, Ben's Eagle shirt.

"I don't believe you," I said back, straight faced.

"I knew I liked something about you," Giuls laughed.

We spent the next hour or so all chatting amongst ourselves and by that, I mean of course, I mostly listened and stared at the way his lips made shapes. I liked the way he said words that began with "m" and "n." I was being a creep. Practice had let out. Kenny came jogging towards us. "Hey Pais, you ready to go?"

"Wait, I'm having a party by my house tonight. You guys should come. Last party before school starts," Ben said.

"Oh yeah, maybe," I offered, knowing I wouldn't actually go.

"Yeah you should come. I'll actually have someone to talk to," Giuls encouraged me.

"Yeah, no, yeah..." I looked to Kenny for help.

"Yeah, yeah we'll come, thanks man," Kenny said. Not the help I was looking for.

"Ok sweet," Ben jumped up. "I'll see you there, Paisley."

"Yeah, ok." I blushed. He wouldn't let go of my eyes. It was like he was trying to see if I was telling the truth or not.

"Alright, let's go get Will before you start drooling on yourself," Giuls said, pulling Ben's arm.

"Ok, I'll see you guys there," Ben said, turning back once more, nearly tripping down the stairs.

Kenny and I looked at one another and broke into laughter. "Who the hell was that?" He asked.

"I don't know," I giggled and shook my head.

"Did you just giggle?" Kenny poked at my ribs trying to tickle me.

"Ok, ok …" I swatted his hands. "No, stop." He poked again. "Kenny, no, no -"

That was Ben. His eyes were green. He was a senior. He smoked cigarettes and weed. He wore the same t-shirt all the time. He was friends with Will and Giuls and he was having a party tonight. I tallied everything I knew about him, memorizing every ounce I could.

---

"Where you guys going?" Mom said from behind us, as Kenny and I slipped on our jackets. She was holding a spatula up with a yellow apron tied around her denim jeans.

"To a party. It's down the block," Kenny said stuffing his arm through a black denim sleeve and walking out the front door.

"Oh, I thought we could all have dinner together before school starts. I'm making pancakes," she frowned, hurt by Kenny's quick exit. Her curls wilted down around her heart shaped, rosy cheeked face. "But that's ok. We can always do another night. You have fun."

"A bunch of the guys on his baseball team are going," I said, apologetically.

"Oh yeah, yeah, go have fun. I'll save you some for the morning."

"We'll probably be back soon," I said, heading for the door.

42

"Oh Paisley -" she called. "You guys will be home tonight, right? Or do you usually stay over a friend's house or you know, like what do you guys do when you go out?"

"We don't have any friends here."

"Oh ok, so you'll be home tonight then?" She asked nervously, careful not to tread through.

"We'll be home later, don't worry," I assured her.

---

It was like walking through a cheap smoke machine. Oxygen replaced secondhand marijuana smoke. The tiled floor sticky with beer, caught a hold of my soles like a mouse trap. Every surface from the fireplace mantle to the very end of the staircase railing was lined with empty blue cans, some carelessly laying on their sides, letting out the dregs. Bodies bordered every wall and edge of furniture. Gritty sounding guitar and crooning deep vocals blared through the standing speakers. Everyone was sitting around, gossiping, running their fingers through their hair, nursing drinks, chugging drinks, floating. I immediately recognized the song blaring through the speakers, crooning, "take me down to the river bend. I wanna be with all my friends…"

"Getting wasted!" The party shouted at once.

"Ha, so this is where everyone is," I said to myself. *This is what they use all the space for.*

"What?" Kenny shouted over the music. "I'm gonna go get a beer. You want one?" He asked walking off. I thought of the day Chris had a fit and started to cry because the elves were stealing his good scotch. Mom and I found out it was Kenny and his boyfriend. We decided to keep it between the two of us. It was a sort of bonding moment, I guess.

The house was greying, but there were no pictures to show times passed, just still life paintings of seagulls and landscapes of beaches and oceans hung on the walls. I tried to find a space somewhere inside the lines of order, but it seemed everyone already had priorly arranged seating.

I made my way through the limbs as I walked up the L- shaped stairs. Trying to find the bathroom, I first opened a closet door, then a door immediately shut back in my face by two girls making out and then finally the bathroom door only to find Ben peeing into the toilet. He looked to me and simply smiled through bloodshot eyes. He was oddly calm, but I guess mostly high. I let out a frazzled very strange foreign (to myself) sound and shut the door as quickly as I could. "Wait, wait Paisley," he shouted from the other side. With astonishing haste, I peeled the corner and rushed down the stairs. I should have run right out of that house.

"Hey Paisley!" Giuls shouted from the bottom.

"Paisley!" Ben shouted from behind me. My neck snapped back and forth at the hollers. "Come on," he said grabbing my hand, "I promised I washed them." His smile was so dorky and bright. It made me tense, like when they show you in science class what particles look like in a solid. He made me nervous, the kind where caterpillars are crawling around the inside of your stomach.

"You came!" Giuls said excitedly. "This is Will."

"What's up?" He nodded. Will was very tall and very traditionally handsome in a boy-ish indie film kind of way. He had short black hair and sparkly blue-green irises that sat in pink veined pools. He was wearing an old Dead Head t-shirt, almost identical to the one Chris wore for two weeks straight. Chris said that they were the greatest band to ever live.

The sound warped in.

"Ben, Ben!" someone shouted over the music. It was Ray. He pulled his hand out of mine.

Giuls must have seen it because she gave me this sort of pity smile. Funny, she hadn't seemed like the comforting type. My ego pulsed in pain. "Come on, let's go outside. It's getting crowded in here." Giuls linked her arm into mine and said, "Will, you coming?' She warded him like leverage. He followed and nodded towards Ben to follow suit.

We went into the backyard, standing around in a circle, passing a joint and when I said, "no thanks," Ben gave me this funny look like I was some prude loser. I didn't care though. I didn't care what people in my high school thought of me last year and I wasn't going to start with some guy who, what, made me a little nervous? *I cared. I really fucking cared.*

"Do you want a drink?" Ben asked me.

"No, I'm good," I lied. I didn't mean it. He intimidated me and I hated it. I pretended to be engaged in the conversation, but the truth is, I couldn't stop staring at Will and Giuls. I know she said they weren't dating but it sure seemed that way. The way he tilted his body towards her, laughed at her dry jokes, cupped his hands around her lighter. It was like this little string of light connected them by the shoulders, flashing each time she touched him. Watching them together was almost addictive, the way it is in movies.

- Paisley? Hello?" Ray waved her hand in front of my face.

"Oh wait, what?" I stuttered. *Dissolve* to Ray's arm in Ben's. Their thread wasn't connecting, it was snipped, short circuiting at the ends, spasming in air. "Sorry, what did you say?"

"Are you joining cheerleading?" She asked.

"Oh," I laughed like it was a joke, but her expression stayed the same. "Oh no, definitely not." The group sort of laughed under their breath, presumably understanding my shock.

"Cheerleading is like the biggest sport here. You're a transfer student, aren't you? You're not here for the athletic programs? What other reason would you come here?" She was rude, just the way I imagined her to be.

"What she means to say is that she's a cheerleader and she wants to know why you're not joining her cult," Giuls said. Ben rolled his eyes at her.

"It's a long boring story," I shrugged my shoulders.

"Well what is it?" She prodded. I looked to Ben, but he looked down to his sneakers. I felt the bugs crawl up my intestines.

"It's not really any of your business," I reflexively spurt out. I hoped no one heard the pause. I panicked. What was I supposed to say? My dead aunt took us from my mom when we were little because she was a raging alcoholic who lost her job but -

"Um ok," she chalked. "Just trying to have a conversation. You don't have to be a weirdo about it."

"Ray," Ben snapped at her.

"Fuck you Ray," Giuls said. "Why don't you go back to your zombies?"

"No, it's cool. I'll be the wierdo." I sipped my drink. I could frost faster than she could near make me melt. "Aren't you supposed to be nice to weirdos or whatever? Cause you know, they're the ones who kill all the cheerleaders."

Ray's jaw twisted at the joint. "What the fuck Ben? Why do you hang out with these people?" She turned as if she was about to storm away, but instead she turned back around waiting for him to follow. He pulled a joint from his shirt-pocket and looked back down to his sneakers. "Fuck you Ben."

"Yeah, yeah fuck me, I know. I'm the asshole," he laughed. Ray's mouth twitched in and out of a frown and she walked off like a wounded child. Unmoved, he looked to his watch for the time and then shouted gallantly, "To the Sump!"

They poured out from the house into the backyard, laughing and running for the fence like a bell had rung through the hallways of the last day of school. They shimmied through openings and jumped at the chain links, helping one another over the fence. Ben, Giuls and Will sort of laughed together in a, "you'll learn," way. And they would teach me. "Come on weirdo," Giuls said grabbing my hand.

Ben walked ahead with another friend, waving his lit joint around by the snap of his wrist, like some kind of androgynous flamboyant rocker who was meant to live in leather with glitter sparkled between the shadow of his ribs for all of eternity. But he didn't, he lived here in dirty sneakers and no one cared about what he did with his wrists but me. They exchanged a small bag and folded cash in a handshake and parted ways. Ben stuffed the bills into his shirt pocket carelessly.

Everyone under the light of the summer crescent moon fit into a panoramic film. All of a sudden, they started to run up ahead. Like an army, the next tier followed suit and then the next. My immediate thought was that they were all running away from something but when I heard their cheers and laughter up ahead, it became clear that they were running because it was finally safe to.

We raced, all of us together, not away or towards something but for it. We ran for the contract of youth, to appease the fire in our limbs, along the carts of trains we'd one day simply either catch or miss, to burn away our adolescent artificially sweetened blood, for the desire to neither shed or gain new layers but to exist happily in our fading beauty, for the lives we had, right there, in that state of bliss. Mind the gap. We ran because the three years of stagnancy and shell that high school had forgiven us was crashing down at the soles of our muddies shoes and that was the one thing, we all had in common. We are the running youth; we are the dead youth and we are coming for you.

*Un joven corriendo, un joven muerto, ellos vienen por ti.*

Whatever version of high school I had clung to suddenly dissipated. It tasted different. We jumped into the virtual chlorine pools, for the baby blue skies, through the soundproof windows, towards the moon that faithfully followed the sun, like everything was alright. Even just for that moment. We are the running youth; we are the dead youth and we are coming for you.

The harboring gloom that lined my perspective eased. I was allowed to be blissful for a short sweet moment. I don't feel I have received many and I dare not be gluttonous with them. I'm glad for however they come and whenever they do decide to go.

*...along the carts of trains, we'd one day simply either catch or miss.*

Hours had quickly passed and somehow, I found myself alone with him. I felt lucky, like he had chosen me. I hated that he could make me feel that way. I looked up and just like that, he was rambling on about what, I had no idea. He said, "the gold wheat liquor had momentarily mollified my murky mind, the gold wheat liquor had momentarily mollified my murky mind, the gold wheat..." He seemed to me then the tallest, brightest, and most beautiful person in the entire world.

"Ok, I've said it three times so we'll remember," he said.

"I think the phrase you're repeating is probably a sign that you won't."

"Well I was repeating it for you, not me," he joked. "So, you don't really drink? Or smoke? Or?"

"I do sometimes," I said shyly. The truth was I had only done either a handful of times because I wasn't very fond of parties. They made me anxious and shaky, out of control. Also, I was never invited to them. My high school party experience consisted of me being the first person out of the building when the bell rung. "Not with people I don't know though."

"Isn't it supposed to be a social thing though? You're always going to be around people you don't know."

"I guess. My aunt gave me that advice though and she said that it was a lesson she learned the hard way. I figure I should try to avoid that."

"That's a good reason then. You should stick with it," he said, firmly. I took his beer from his hand. It tasted awful.

"Does that mean you think you know me, now?"

"It means I want to," I said bravely. He just stood there with that same buzzy grin. I could have said something about how his words felt musical and he made me so nervous that I could feel little air bubbles in my bloodstream, but I didn't. I was murky and he stood there blazing like the sun at night. He seemed so whole and I was running on empty. "But I have to get home. I'm gonna head out."

"If you want, I can walk you," he mumbled.

"No, no it's cool, my house is right there."

"No, I mean I want to walk you. And if you're gonna go, I might as well too." I almost giggled out of nervousness but instead I quickly looked away and focused on the foul aftertaste of warm beer to curb it.

"I like your wrists," I blurted out.

*...the gold wheat liquor had momentarily mollified my murky mind.*

"Thanks, like the song?" he said curiously, inspecting his arms.

I nodded yes.

"I like that one too... I like your wrists too."

# 6

# "Oh, fuck yeah French fries."

"P ais wake up," Kenny said, hovering above me the next morning.

"What, what happened?" I woke in a panic.

"That guy Ben is asleep outside on the stoop." I stared back confused, swatting at the morning in my eyes. "He's just sleeping there. I don't know if he's like dead, or something."

"That's not funny Kenny," I said pulling a sweater over my head, aggravated.

Ben was sleeping on the front steps in the same clothes from last night with his face against the stone. I crouched down, shook his arm and whispered, "Ben, Ben wake up." He snapped his head up so fast I heard his neck crack back into place.

\*\*\*

Ben sat at the kitchen island with his head between his arms, eyelids stretched pink, inhaling steam from the cup of coffee. I slid ibuprofen towards him.

"What the shit.... I guess I just never went home when I dropped you off." His grubby fingers wrapped around the mug. "Fuck," he laughed to himself. I picked out a leaf from his hair. "Thanks." He swallowed the pills down.

Mom strutted into the kitchen in a tank and boxers. "Well good morning, good morning. Who's this?" She said, throwing her arms around my shoulders, dragging out her vowels.

"This is Ben." I said.

"Well hello Ben, I'm Gina. Paisley's mom. And you know, you're welcome here whenever you want, but it's a little early so I'm gonna go ahead and assume you took a morning jog here for coffee... (her hair expanded like territory). It's nice to see you making friends so quickly." Mom smushed her dry lips into my cheek.

"That's your mom?" Ben said laughing. "She's hot." I dug my face into my hands. She might have been taking the "mom" thing a bit too far. I forgot how young she must have looked compared to the other moms in town.

"So that's it, huh? No questions about how I ended up sleeping on your front lawn?" He asked.

"Hm... well do you wanna talk about it?"

"Um well, no I guess not," he shook his head.

"Well that settles that," I said. I knocked my wrists together. He just stared at me blankly, his eyes looking more like an opaque koi pond, but still beautiful in the morning light. He squeezed my hand and smiled sadly. Maybe he wasn't as whole and entire as I painted him. "So what time is it?

"I think around seven, I don't know."

"What are you doing today?" He asked me sweetly.

"Like today, as in right now? Nothing, I don't know anyone here," I quipped.

"Great," he grinned triumphantly and headed for the side door. "Come on, I wanna show you something. Go put on your sneakers."

He grabbed my hand and headed for the sump. We were running. Again. I pieced together that people from the suburbs enjoyed moving fast when they got the chance. He pulled me down into the bush. "Ben there are bugs and snakes in here and stuff," I said swatting my hand in front of my face.

Cliche sugar - he softly brushed a loose strand of hair behind my ear. "Come on, look. Wait for it," he whispered and took my hand back into his. "Wait for it..." He squeezed tightly. I stared on dough eyed.

Suddenly, two girls came piling out of the hedges gripping cans of beer and tripping over the uneven ground. One by one, people came shooting out from far corners of the sump like a pinball machine. Their arms chained together, laughing hysterically, feet storming through the golden summer weeds. "Ok, you ready? You gotta run fast. That's the rules."

"Wait, what?" Without explanation, he ripped at my arm and booked it.

We spurted through the field, almost colliding with someone heading straight for our bush, their arms wrapped around an orange water cooler. "Come on, come on!" He shouted. Trails of morning light sparkled through the green branches above us and the morning heat whipped through my t-shirt. Our elongated shadows shot behind us and pieces of broken glass twinkled like gems. The only sound came from echoed cheerful laughter and our sneakers skidding on the gravel.

When we reached the other side of the field, it felt as if only seconds had passed. He looked back at me, weak lunged, trying to catch his breath and said, "not bad."

We crawled back into his yard through a ripped piece of the chain link fence.

Giuls and Will sat in plastic white chairs on the wooden deck. "You're late," Giuls said flicking her joint into the lawn. "But you brought Paisley, so you're forgiven."

"Nice to see you too Giuls," Ben said.

---

"I don't get it," I laughed picking up an empty cup and tossing it into a garbage bag.

"Those are the rules. If you wanna get through the sump in the morning. The rules are, you run as fast as you can through the sump, and no one says a word. It's like you were never there. It's a pact." Will said.

"But why do you have to have never been there?" I asked, already regretting my blaringly green, innocent question.

"Well if you're running through the sump in the morning... it means you probably did something you don't want someone to know about last night." Giuls interjected. I thought to myself how Ben must have not wanted anyone to know about him waking up on my stoop or about us being together now. It made sense.

"That and free beer," Will added.

"It's a tradition. It's called the Sump Sprint. They've been doing it since the 60's." Ben corrected Will with almost a sense of patriotism.

I imagined the decades of youth running hand in hand through the field, all the same footprints stepped in, how the patterns embossed into rubber changed from decade to decade. I wondered if Chris was one of the pairs of feet or if he had always locked himself away in his bedroom.

### The Sump Sprint

"That's pretty cool. And this? Cleaning up? Is that some kind of tradition?" I said, fluffing a couch pillow.

"Yep. We traditionally keep Ben from getting his ass kicked for throwing parties," Giuls said.

"So, he can throw more. Who wants a shot?" Will said walking through the doorway with a bottle of dark colored liquor in his hand.

"Depends what you got," Giuls said, with a kiddish smirk. She passed the bottle to Ben who took a swig and wiped at his mouth with the back of his hand. Will picked the bottle back up and asked me, "you wanna kill it?" I took a swig and winced at the flavor. Whiskey. Ben offered a smile of approval, like I had passed some initiation test.

"I was saving that, you know?" A boy with black curly hair said from the stairs.

"My bad Rex," Will took the blame. He lifted up the four loaded garbage bags by their strings.

"Alright, we're pulling out. You ready babe?" Will said to Giuls, discomfort in his tone.

"Yeah, let's go. Pais, you good? You want a ride anywhere?" She lifted the last remaining bag.

"I'm good," I smiled. I liked Giuls, which was strange, but mostly because I could tell she liked me too. Which was strange. She was honest and bold without being precocious. For whatever reason, she had extended an arm towards me and I was trying to reach back. It was the first time I ever wanted to. I wasn't sure if I was doing it right.

Ben walked with them out towards the back door. Rex came down from the stairs and said sweetly, "I'm Rex." His voice was delicate, feminine. His charm reminded me of Ben. "You're new. Ken's sister, right? Paisley?" They looked mostly alike except that Rex had all the dominant features; dark hair, dark eyes, tanner skin. His shoulders pulled back gracefully, poised.

"Yeah," I said, shortly. It figured Kenny introduced himself already. Rex was beautiful and Kenny moved on fast. I'd give it two days before he was at the foot of my bed chewing my ear off about Ben's cute brother. It was our thing. He was always the one with all the boy problems.

"Except for the beer & cigarette smell, I think you guys did pretty good this time around. Aggie won't notice a thing." I knew the scent and I could read between the lines. *Aggie was a drunk.*

"Will seems good," Rex said beyond me.

"Yeah, you know, good as he can be," Ben said, reaching for my hand. "Are you heading out?"

"I think I might stay a little longer... you know, make sure Aggie doesn't kill you before Senior year even starts." Rex smirked and went back up the stairs. It felt like a medieval exchange of family secrets.

---

Ben and I went upstairs to his room, it being the only place that "didn't smell bad." We sat at the edge of his bed. Ben reached for an ibuprofen bottle and swallowed down more without any water.

"Do you mind if I have one of those?" I asked.

"Oh yeah, yeah. There's more downstairs. I'll go get you some." He ran out the door, but peaked back in and said grinning, "with water!" Mind reader.

*I'm not freaking out. I'm fine. This is fine.*

He came back in and sat down beside me again, watching intently (very weirdly) as I took another sip of water. "Do you want some?" I laughed, spilling a bit on myself.

"Nah, you have it," he said, smiling brightly.

Our fingers laid gently beside one another, like bridges with missing planks.

"So, who's Aggie?" I asked cautiously.

"Oh yeah, Aggie. She's our Aunt. I kinda live with her, but she's never really here. She's always on cruises. She took us in when our parents died and... yeah, you know." He suddenly clawed his hand into mine, squeezing his fingers into the balls of my knuckles. I felt the sad beryl dye come through his wrists and into my fingertips, igniting the frozen over ends that once touched Aunt Nadine.

"I didn't realize that both of your parents... that they-"

"Yeah, it's shitty," he looked towards the window. "But I just have one more year and then, I think it'll get easier once I leave. My mom used to say that you couldn't heal in the same places that hurt you, that it was like trying to walk the same path when you already knew it was covered in broken glass. I don't know."

59

"I get it. She sounds really smart." Careful to not put her in the past tense.

"Yeah and really funny, like - really funny."

He was a teenager when it happened so he could remember everything about his mother which, "makes it harder. Like I wish it happened when I was little or something. I don't know if that makes a difference." I told him I thought it did, but that it was just hard in a different way. And then I told him that, "I never talked about my father with anyone like this before."

He said his mother always smelled like lavender, that her voice was dark and confident because of all the cigarettes she smoked. And that he could remember how his father would say his name from down the stairs and sometimes he could still hear him like tinnitus in his ear. They were coming back from a party in Jersey when it happened, when their car wrapped around a tree. After that with no other options, Aggie took Ben and Rex in, but he said she never liked the two of them very much.

Rex came back for the summer, but besides that Ben was pretty much on his own. Ben's scars were far more tender than he led on. I tried to imagine us as two things that fit together, but it made me wonder if two empties could ever fill one another. We were two key holes, two hollows, two bottles, two purple suitcases. How would we fill up? Could we ever? Did a person do that to you? How do you know when it's happening and if it's a good thing or not?

"Paisley?" Ben asked. "You ok?"

"Oh shit, sorry, yeah I'm fine."

He grabbed my face into his hands and kissed gently at my mouth. He tasted like cigarettes and coffee. He pushed his lips into mine firmly once more with his thumb pressed into the hollow of my cheek. Then I thought that maybe he felt it too, that he knew exactly where I went, that he was there too. Where do we go when our minds wander off? Where did they go when they went away? Were they in the same places? Were we all there together?

It felt like only minutes, but the hours rolled by and he held my hands tightly like I would have floated off without him. Our mouths bled together, the room fogged and blushed. We laid on his bed with our limbs and veins tangled, letting the clock's arms circle. It was like deja vu. I had been there before. When his arms wrapped around me - they were returning, not arriving. I trusted him. I felt safe, the kind that isn't taken away but ripped. The kind of rip that leaves you mangled. He would smile and then kiss my lips and then smile and then kiss my cheek and every single time I felt nervous that I was doing something incorrectly. "What?" He would ask playfully, and I would nod confused again. "You're funny Paisley," he teased.

He went to press his face into my neck when another knock came from the door. "Yo." It was Will. Ben groaned, kissed my cheek one last time, then hollered back, "Yeah come in."

Giuls and Will walked through the door with bags of fast food. "Oh, fuck yeah French fries," Ben said sitting up on his elbows.

They both came in and sat right down on the bed with us. It all felt so normal, like I was fitting into something that was waiting for me. Like it was already mine.

# 7

# Daydream *

 "Let's get knee deep into it, shall we? Welcome to CLK Miss. Ciel."

Mrs. Skela's hair was dyed an artificial fire engine red and she wore a matching pant suit, sleek like a devil's costume in a movie. Miles long, claw-like nails tapped lightly against the oak desk. It was like a circus tent talking. Though even through the scarlet charade, you could tell that her smile was not the same color as her costume.

"Thanks," I said plainly.

I hated being called Miss. I hated the same itchy fabric on the chairs, the creaked open window, the gold thumbtacks on green fabric walls, the maroon carpet, the parched dying flowers hanging from a planter on the window frame. Why do all guidance counselor offices have the same smell to them? Like something was dying inside of them. Mr. Salem's floating head appeared, shaking at me in disapproval. *Hard to judge with no spine, huh? I said to him.*

Her office was surprisingly barren, like she had just arrived today. A picture frame facing towards her, a stapler, a notebook and a lemon on her desk. In that order.

"Ok well, I'm Mrs. Skela and I'm your guidance counselor. I wanna know you, the whole deal. Goals in life, dream-school, hobbies, extracurriculars, all that. Where do we start? Tell me something about you."

"I just moved here." When her hand moved under her chin, I saw her engagement ring, a giant sapphire, surrounded by a crest of sparkling rubies. I wondered if her partner wore blue.

"Alright, well that's a good place to start? What are some of your hobbies when you're spending alone time with yourself?" She was trying to be optimistic. I felt a little bad, but then I thought of the way her door would eventually be closed.

"I don't know. I like writing sometimes, I guess."

"And that's all the time we have. Next!" She shouted like a mail clerk, then breaking into laughter. I leaned back and looked out the window. "Ok, bad joke. Good to know. Crossing it off. This feels awkward, but it shouldn't be. Why don't we start over fresh tomorrow and you can tell me how today goes? Same time?"

"That's ok. I probably have a lot of homework and stuff that I should do. I think I pretty much have the hang of it, you know the bells and stuff and yeah…" I lied.

"Ok then, I'll be here whenever you feel like dropping in. Don't forget we have our monthly check-in!" She smiled brightly.

"Um ok," I said waving goodbye. She was weird. I liked her, a little bit.

\*\*\*

Empty hallway lined with pastel green tile from floor to tippy tops of wall. Lockers - navy blue, so worn, they looked more like broken in denim than rust covered with paint. With a blink, papers flew in the air. Fluorescent lights above dashed like lines on a highway. Hyena laughter filled the airwaves and you could hear the one-track mind as if it were blasting through like a main-office announcement. High school is a dance of the contagion, the chemicals from a periodic table doing a sloppy, two left footed waltz. "Weirdo," said the announcement speakers. Again, and again. *Weirdo, Weirdo, Weirdo.*

- "miss, do you have somewhere to be?" An older stout woman with silver, fine hair said to me. I opened my eyes. It was empty again and I could breathe.

"I'm lost. I'm new," I fell over my words.

"Can I see your schedule?" she said like a grumpy dwarf. I handed her my crinkled schedule from my jean pocket. "You need to be in the gymnasium. That's the first floor, but you're on the other side of the building."

"I'll help her Miss," Ben said from behind me. "I'm going that way anyway." The woman shook her head indifferently and hobbled off in her orthopedic sneakers snarling something inaudible.

"Are you following me now?" I laughed. He grabbed my backpack and slung it over his shoulder. My stomach flipped. His eyes were evergreen today, rimmed in a faint pink, veins branching through his lids. He always looked so tired. Maybe he was just always high.

"Yes, yes I am actually. I don't know why you've only just noticed," he laughed. "I called your name like three times...where's your head today?"

"I don't know," I sighed sadly and smiled. "I think it's broken."

He laughed like it was a joke, but we both knew it wasn't.

We walked side by side through the morning crowd of jubilant teenagers, jammed in like fish caught in a net, sparkling eyes, heads turned, "*who is that?*", mouths gaping, "*Ray is gonna freak out.*"

A path cleared for Ben Rosen, with his one arm swinging to the rhythm of his words and the other reaching behind him to pull the *who is that* girl through. *How did they know already? What did they know already? High school is like the movies, but only the bad parts.*

People smiled as they caught his eye and then gazed on curiously, like he wasn't one of them. It was a town of molds and the monster of a cement truck drove right by his home. He roamed freely through the grid line, unnoticed and unearthed and it freaked the living hell out of everyone around him. I could see that people were scared of him, not because of something he did, but because of something in him. And whatever that something was, it made them uncomfortable with themselves. But he was near me, so it was all ok. He held my hand on my first day of Senior year, where I somehow managed to become the *visible girl.*

"Ok I'll see you in a little," he said gently pulling his hand away. He pointed towards the gym.

"Wait, where are you going?" I asked nervously.

"I have to go to the boy's locker room. You have to go into the girl's," he smiled, pointing to the split entrances. "You want me to walk you to the locker room?"

I nodded yes. I didn't want him to go. I didn't want to be here alone. "Don't listen to them, ok? I won't either. They don't matter. Because they don't get it."

---

The girl's locker room had a top value placed on how little space there was between your skin and your bone. Stomachs caved in towards hips. Breasts were pushed up high towards the neck with wires and cushion.

Ray was at the far-left corner of the room, laughing amongst her group of velour friends. When she caught me staring, I expected her to charge for me, but instead she plainly rolled her eyes and let off a resonant frown that could not be hid behind a buckled grin.

She knew. I had hurt her. It wasn't because I disliked her. I mean I did dislike her, but I didn't take him away on purpose because of it. It doesn't matter why you hurt someone though, does it? The only thing that matters is that you did it. All the reasoning and explanations in the world can't take back the pain you caused or remove yourself as the source of it. What's worse is that a small part of me felt good about what I did. I wondered what kind of person that made me or if it just made me like everybody else.

It made me believe I deserved the karma that came next. I grabbed the wrong bag of clothes. Instead of a gym uniform, I had a massive (and I mean massive) t-shirt with a wolf on it and sweatpants I needed to roll five times to get them somewhere near my waist. *Who the hell would wear this anywhere? Right. Chris.*

Class was separated by gender and into four quadrants. Half of the grade took gym while the other half of the grade took health class and the schedules swapped every other day. Most students were athletes who wore their uniforms and looked forward to this period, but physical education for most people (normal people) was a gauntlet, a fleshy unmonitored opportunity for some asshole with neanderthal humor to throw a basketball at your head.

The gym's wooden floor mirrored the colors of the room, the maroon and gold banners hanging down from the ceiling rafters, the scoreboard zeroed out. It was cathedral-like, missing its podium. Teenagers with lanky limbs huddled together for comfort.

"Wait, what the hell are you wearing?" Giuls laughed from behind me. "Is that a wolf on your shirt?" The other girls walked out one by one, pointing and snickering at me.

"Yes," I said palming my face. "I didn't, I didn't realize -" I stuttered.

"What? That other people would be at school?" She said, through her laughter. Her face sort of pinched up and she murmured, "Ben's coming."

"What is that on your shirt?" Ben tugged at the bottom of my shirt. "A wolf, huh?" He and Giuls laughed together. My face flooded with steam.

"Did they not tell you about the gym uniform?" Giuls asked.

"I grabbed the wrong bag, obviously," I said, as a whistle sounded. I put my face back into my hands.

"I think you look cute," he said, then kissing my cheek. My stomach flipped. He jogged back over to the boys. When I turned around, Ray was there blank faced and fuming. Giuls just continued laughing. I realized then, she must have been high too. Was everyone just high all the time?

* * *

"Don't worry, it'll all blow over soon." Giuls said jogging by my side.

"What are you talking about?" I said out of breath, feeling my freshly inked dress-code detention slip crumpled in my pocket.

"Your shirt. And Ray. She won't do anything. She'll just talk a lot of shit. Don't worry. She hates me way more than she hates you," she said. We both stopped, out of breath, resting our hands on our knees. There was a trophy and plaque display. It was filled with gold medals and mementos and pictures of a boy who looked like Will. For a second I thought it was him.

"Hey, who is that in there?" I asked pointing towards it.

"Oh yeah, that *was* Will's older brother, Weston." Her voice dropped an octave and the color flushed out of the room. "He died a couple of summers ago on a sailing trip. They never found the boat. He had a full ride to NYU and everything. The whole town threw this huge memorial for him. It was really sad."

"I had no idea," I said remorsefully.

"Yeah Will doesn't talk about it. But he doesn't really talk about anything."

"What do you mean? You guys don't talk about anything?"

"No, not really," she shrugged. We started back up. "He doesn't really say much. We just have like sex and stuff. I mean he's a really good listener, but he just doesn't have much to say. Sometimes he says he loves me, but I don't know. I can't tell what he really means by it, you know?"

My heart felt for Will, the boy whose words were plastered to the side of a sailboat lost somewhere in the water. "Yeah, I think so," I said.

Ben started to jog towards us. "Hey, hey," he said with his arms halfheartedly pumping up and down from his sides.

"Hi," I said back, in my *dumb fucking* wolf shirt.

"What are you doing after school today?" Ben asked.

---

We all sprawled out on the carpet in Ben's basement. As it turns out, in addition to having all the unsupervised house parties, Ben was also the town's favorite flower boy too. He was the reason half of the school spent their days high out of their mind. He said it was the only reason people were so nice to him all the time; "hoping for free weed, I guess." Being in the house felt like being in a 70's time warp, but it smelled like an old closet. "I feel like I'm in an old TV show right now," Will laughed. Maybe we all compared our lives to glass screens.

"Ok, my turn. What's everyone doing after senior year?" Giuls asked.

Ben, Will and I all looked at one another, smirked and then started shouting "boo" at her. That was how the game worked. The premise was "no bad question," but it was really called <u>The Game</u> and you were only allowed to ask about topics that we could all get lost in, riff off, dive into. It wasn't a very original title, but it was to the point. If you asked a stupid question, you got booed because you sucked at asking questions. Fair enough.

When the joint made its way to me, I looked up at Ben to find his sight already fixed on me. I inhaled, knowing I was only smoking to gain some sense of approval from him, but not caring about anything other than it. As pathetic as it sounded, I would have done just about anything for him already, to be near him, to be called by him, to gain his heart. When I exhaled without a hitch, I was proud of myself for not breaking into a coughing fit. He seemed relieved. Like I had passed again.

"I've got one," I said. "There's this word. Schadenfreude. It means like…like when you get pleasure from seeing something bad happening to someone. Do you think feeling that makes you a bad person?" I couldn't stop thinking about Ray and the way I derived a sense of pleasure from knowing that I had hurt her back.

"Everyone experiences that. We can't all be bad people. It's like watching the bad guy get killed off. Everyone experiences some kind of pleasure from that," Ben said. *Ugh, his curls. I sound so gross, but his eyes. I think I'm high.*

"Maybe that just means we all have the capability of being bad people. Doing bad things doesn't make you a bad person," Will said, inhaling. They all looked so cool whenever they took a hit. I needed to catch up.

"I don't know, it made me really happy to see Ray's jaw drop today in gym. It made my day," Giuls said. *That's retribution, it doesn't count*, I thought.

"Don't be an asshole Giuls," Ben scolded.

"Alright whatever, whatever. There has to be some kind of point system. My dad is a bad person, He knows it. I know it. He deserves bad things to happen to him and I don't feel like a bad person for that. When my mom kicked him out, she threw all of his clothes out the window *AND* she smashed his Benz windshield in with a bat. Oh! And then, and then," she laughed, "She snapped all of his cigars in half. He was sobbing like a baby and I couldn't stop laughing. Karma happens, it doesn't absolve us in the process." I would later learn that Giuls always laughed when she was high, often inappropriately.

"Shit," Ben said blank faced. Will's chest cavity inflated as he nervously readjusted himself.

"Is that how you really feel about him?" I chimed in.

71

"Yeah, yeah it is." Giuls abruptly stopped laughing and spoke with her chin in the air, clinging to her hurt. She was lying.

"Ok, I have one, I have one," Will interjected. Giuls seemed grateful for the interruption. "Shrimp have the most color cones in their eyes."

"That's not a question," Giuls said. We all exploded into another fit of laughter.

Even as practical strangers, we all felt it, how special it was, the energy between us, the lightness in our skelatons after laughing so thunderously, thinking what we thought to be so boldly, how much fun it was to play pretend, like we were the next great thinkers of the world. It was special. It was decided. We would all walk home from school together and come back to play the game tomorrow and the day after that and the day after that. We all stuck around, for as long as we could. When the game came to an end for the day, it was time to leave.

"You need a ride?" Giuls asked me smirking. Will had already left without saying goodbye.

"I'll give her one." Ben jumped in, before I could respond.

I didn't understand what Giuls meant about Will not talking. He seemed ok with talking during the game. At the party, it seemed like Giuls was the only person his circuits really connected to. Maybe things were different when they were alone together. Sure, he was quiet but not in an alarming way. I wondered what it was like between them all before I was here.

Ben had convinced me to stay a little while longer, though I didn't need much persuasion. All I wanted was to be near him. Wherever he was, that was where I wanted to be. *You are where I like to be. Always, Always.* To think that he felt the same filled me with electricity. I pulled myself onto the kitchen counter, kicking my knees into a cross. Ben stepped in towards me. "So how was your first day?" he mused, bright eyed, rubbing his hands over my knees. There was this hunk of metal in my lungs and he was the magnet. I was hopelessly drawn to the physical phenomenon implanted in his bones.

"Well it was school - so it sucked. And then I wore a wolf t-shirt in front of everyone in my high school, and I'm pretty sure everyone already hates me so it could have gone better actually," I said, sarcastically.

"I think you looked cute," he said, picking a joint and lighter out of his shirt pocket. He took a pull and passed me the joint. I loved watching him inhale and exhale smoke, the embers catch, his shoulders lifting and dropping. *Lava.*

"Your aunt is just never here? You can just do whatever you want all the time in this giant house?" I asked.

"Yeah pretty much." His lids squinted through glazed irises. I wrapped my legs around his torso, the way I had seen girls do on TV, and pressed my lips into his mouth. "I'm really happy you're here Paisley," he said boldly. He looked at me through the clouds.

"Oh yeah?" I smirked.

"Yeah, yeah I am," he giggled, sweetly. "You want me to say it again or something?"

"Yeah I do." I bit down on the inside of my cheek to keep my composure.

"I'm really, really happy you're here."

"...and?" I added. "You didn't say the best part."

"Paisley?" I nodded. "Oh, yes. I'm really, really happy you're here Paisley."

"Again," I demanded, laughing and dug my face into his neck.

"Paisley, Paisley, Paisley-

It was getting late and I should have gone home by then. We went back upstairs to his bedroom and just laid down talking on his bed for hours, like the last time. I don't even remember what we talked about. But it was *so* funny. It felt like my chest was opening up for the first time – to make more room for oxygen, but instead he filled it up with oxytocin. *Close enough.* He had his Dad's old record player and collection that he was adding to shortly and sweetly. When 'Daydream' played, he sang the chorus to me, because it was the only part he knew, and I sang the verses because I knew every word.

*You're the reason flowers were made.*

My fingertips tingled, like the memory was storing itself away. My cleft made room for his anchor and so came the feeling of missing him as if he were already gone.

Staring through the skylight above my bed, I wondered how a person you've only just met can feel like the only person who really knows who you are. There was a trick at play, a wire to be cut, a branch to be swept from beneath my feet. I would kill to believe - and I mean really believe with every ounce of my being and porous nature that everything happens for a reason, that his existence was retribution for Aunt Nadine's lack of, but then I remembered she was gone, and nothing would make up for it.

Usually I felt clogged up with all these words and thoughts I couldn't make sense of. I couldn't pick which one to feel first. But with Ben's existence came a choice to be happy – I chose to think about how Ben told me that we lived eleven minutes away from one another. I thought of how being high with him was the best feeling in the entire world. And his rippled green eyes and our laughter rumbling in our chests like thunder, cracking the grey sky and all that light pouring out from the fractured lines.

# The Inconsolables *

It had only been a few months in the new house when Chris left for the first time. It was after him and mom had a really bad fight over him drinking so much (a fight I would come to understand was as timely as daylight savings). Muffled screams came from the basement, the sound of glass shattering, an inaudible terrible cry. Kenny burst through the door to find Chris gripping one side of his bloodied face. Mom said it was an accident. Not the part where she threw a bottle at his head. "I meant to do that." But the part where the bottle was already cracked and cut open his cheek. "He'll be back," she said.

"Yeah cause it's his house," Kenny scoffed and stormed off.

"It's fine Kenneth. He'll be back," Mom said, biting at her already chewed fingers. "He'll be back. You know how he gets Pais. Don't worry baby. He'll be back." Her eyes began to leak. I placed my arms around her and mechanically squeezed.

"Yeah mom, he'll be back," I reflexively said. Her hair flattened out and she began to heave sobs into my chest. Aunt Nadine whispered into my ear, "All that energy, well it needs to go somewhere, it's just got to." I pictured all of Mom's sadness leaking into me like dye bleeding into cloth. Like she was contagious, and I was unfortunately spongey and cream colored. I could feel her disease starting to weave into my genes. All the bleach in the world wouldn't be able to scrub it out. But I held her anyways. I held her until she got all of the blue out of her system and I was drenched in it. I went to Ben's house afterwards and he told me that I looked so sick that my skin looked green and I said, "Blue, it looks blue."

"Yeah you're right, it does kinda look blue," he agreed, handing me a glass of ginger ale. We didn't talk about it. I thought about telling him, I did, but I didn't want to get any blue on his skin. It was my blue now to harbor and not to give.

I tried to talk to Kenny about it, but he just said to leave it alone, that he wanted, "to be a fucking normal teenager for once." He was angry and he wouldn't let me hold him anymore. "I don't need you to take care of me anymore Pais. Just go hangout with your boyfriend and your friends."

"He's not my boyfriend," I yelled back, baffled at his aggression.

---

For the first time in my life, school became a place I actually wanted to be. I just wanted to be with my friends. All I thought about during class was being able to see Ben and hold his hand even if it was for just five minutes. We always found a way to spend the breaks between classes together. After that, all I could think about was being able to sit down at lunch with Ben, Will and Giuls. And then after lunch, all I thought about was going back to Ben's house and playing the game. The only time my brain worked was when I was playing the game, when we were asking questions we cared about knowing the answer to. Sometimes we never figured it out and that was the best kind of question. Weed made music feel heavier and meaningful, like it was hiding all of those answers in it. Every day we walked a little bit faster home from school, and we smoked just a little bit more than the last time. We would spin the same record over and over again on the old Victrola and laugh and crawl around the carpets like it was the safest place in the world. The house had already taken on a life of its own. I could feel it breathing, feeding us words like a ventriloquist. It wanted us there, for us to stay, to give it a reason to live again. Like the giving tree, it was becoming a being to return to, to give comfort, to give shelter. It was speaking, singing, dancing around our existence. It was a *thing* that was trying to keep us there so it could protect us the way our parents couldn't. And we felt it, we felt it every time. We gave it, *her,* a name. Linda.

"Linda, we're home," Ben shouted into the empty hallways. Aggie was on a cruise in the arctic. Rex was back in the city. Our parents started to call his house to ask where we were. We spent our time mostly on the floors, but always in different rooms of the house. We sat face to face in the hallways, laying down on blankets and pillows in front of the TV, laying out in the grass. We all liked the ground, the comfort of loose muscles and stretched limbs.

Ben began to refer to us as *The Inconsolables*, like the song. *Calling all sad souls, we are The Inconsolables. All I've ever really learned of love is that it's never yours.*

None of us knew how to play instruments besides him but he said we weren't any less of a band for it. We booed him, but it stuck anyway. We all began to refer to ourselves as The Inconsolables, scribbling the words on notebooks and the plastic of binders and finished tests turned over on our desks.

Will and Giuls would leave, but I would always stay behind to be with Ben. We did what we always did, we smoked and laid on his bed and ate junk food and just talked and talked until I would have to leave. Each time he would beg me to stay the night and each time I almost did. He said he didn't like the air when I wasn't there, that his head began to ache the second I left. I would roll my eyes and pretend that he was kidding.

Ben was so smart and I don't think anyone even realized it. Not even him. There was always a new book on his bedside table, next to the same empty ibuprofen bottle and half full glass of water. He loved reading more than anything in the world, proclaiming that his mother was a "reader", so he was a reader, like it was some kind of secret identity he kept safely. But not from me. We started reading the books together in bed, taking turns flipping the pages. He said, "a good reader, makes a good writer." So, then we began to read my metaphoric scribblings together too. He said a good writer was able to build a universe that made you question why you lived in yours.

At night I would have dreams about him. In them, he tore at my clothing and kissed at my pelvis. I would wake each morning dripping in sweat and blushed. Then I would walk outside of my house and there he was waiting for me with a grin across his face - like he knew. Of course, he didn't, but it made my cheeks rush with blood and he would ask, "why are you looking at me like that?" as he pulled a joint out from his shirt pocket. Oh, and he only wore shirts with front pockets on school days. Every other day, he wore his yellow Ben's Eagle t-shirt. It belonged to his dad.

"So that's pretty exciting, huh? First big senior party of the year at a new school. Maybe you could write about it. You know in just a couple of years, I'll bet you get a real kick out of it." Mrs. Skela said. She was dressed in red head to toe, the way she always was.

"I guess so. I haven't really been writing a lot lately though."

"Why not?" She asked.

"I don't know. I've been busy," I shrugged.

"Ok so I'm gonna give it to you uncomfortably straight. You are the *thee* only Senior in this school that hasn't applied to a single college. Did you know that? The only one."

"I mean obviously I didn't know that," I slid back into my seat.

"Paisley, I think you're a really special girl," she said. "You get straight A's, but you won't speak a word to any of your teachers who also say you don't talk to any of the other kids in your classes school besides Ben Rosen. Your English teacher gave me this paper you wrote." She placed it down on the desk.

"That's not true. I talk to Giuls and Will too," I tallied.

She ignored my comment. "She says that she thought you were going to be a promising student. Did you know that? It says right here on the back of this paper to go see her after school and you didn't. Why not Paisley?"

"I don't know why. I was busy or I don't know, I couldn't even read her handwriting. I mean I got an A. I don't see why I have to go to talk to her about it," I said, flustered.

"Paisley, I know that you love your friends. You light up when you talk about them and Ben. And that is so great and I'm so happy you have found that, but you can't just ignore what's wrong. Eventually, all of the bad things are going to catch up and you're going to be the only one who faces those repercussions."

"Ok, I get it. Can I go now?" Maybe it wasn't the mature thing to do, but I didn't want to talk to some lady dressed like a tomato about my future.

"Yes, you can go." I could tell she was disappointed in me and I liked her I did, but she didn't understand. "One more thing Paisley...your younger brother is down here in my office all the time saying he doesn't know how to talk to you anymore. Maybe you should invite him to the party tonight."

"Wait, what? Kenny is down here saying that? He's the one who stopped talking to me!"

"Yeah, well maybe you should go talk to him then!" she shouted back at me.

"What is going on? You're not allowed to tell me what another student says?" I said angrily.

"Yeah well you're not allowed to walk around being a big old jerk to everyone for no reason."

"Did you just call me a big old jerk? Aren't you not allowed to say that to a student?" I couldn't help but laugh between my words.

81

"Why are you laughing?" She asked, bewildered.

"Because, because - I don't know. It's funny." Because I was high. I was *really* high.

\*\*\*

"Why are you telling the school counselor that you can't talk to me anymore. You're the one who doesn't want to talk to me!" I yelled through Kenny's door.

"Go away!" He yelled back.

"No, why would you do that? Why would you lie like that?" I waited for his response. The door swung open and he stepped out furiously.

"First of all, I am not lying. Second - because you're always with your weirdo boyfriend. When am I supposed to talk to you when you're always with him? It's like he's obsessed with you. When am I supposed to find time to talk to you, huh? Should I call his house too like mom asking you to come home for the dinner she's been trying to make for you for a month now?"

"He is not obsessed with me!"

"Oh God, that's what you hear. You're always over there and you're just leaving me here! Mom and I have had dinner every night together. She's really trying hard Paisley! Did you notice that? Oh, and I got a job too. Did you notice that? No, you didn't because your weird drug dealer boyfriend pays for everything for you! Must be really nice to just not need anything from anyone anymore!"

"That's not fair. You've had like ten boyfriends. I get one and you freak out like a jealous baby!"

"I thought you said he wasn't your boyfriend!" He slammed his bedroom door closed.

"He's not my boyfriend!" I shouted back, kicking the wooden door too hard.

"Good to know Paisley," Ben said, from down the stairs.

I grabbed at my foot in pain and chased down after him. Will, Giuls and Mom stood still in silence in the kitchen. The front door slammed shut. "Your friends are here," Mom said, through pressed lips and strained shoulders. Her cheeks blazed with embarrassment.

"Great," I pronounced.

---

Cue Lolita's mansion. I had never seen such unnecessarily high ceilings. They said it was the biggest house in Old Westbury and that when Ray's older sister got lip injections, her mom made everyone else (including her brothers and father) get them too so that it looked like a naturally inherited trait.

Bodies grinded against the wall and people were shouting into nothingness, badlands oblivion. I felt wings pounding from my side, a flight response. Giuls squeezed at my arm and yelled into my ear, "Don't worry, he'll get over it! You don't have to be anything he doesn't want you to be!"

The party would go down in history as one of the best parties of Senior year. Flash after flash, the night documented by disposable cameras and flip phones. Then from a cloud of smoke an older blonde, rather plump woman walked out. She introduced herself to Giuls and I as Ray's mother. She said, "Don't worry, I'm the cool chaperone. I'm the type of mom who would rather all the kids be close to home when making bad decisions." She burst out with a cackle. Her lips did look a little funny.

Giuls and I just nodded and smiled. She sounded like an accessory to murder in the making and to Giuls, she might as well have been. Ray's mom told the entire town about Giuls' father's affair. When they found out who it was, Will went and smashed her car windows in. She didn't press charges though and no one really talked about it again.

Ben descended down the staircase in jeans and another shirt with a packed pocket (It was going to be a big night for him). He was the creator of the cliche, the valentine of a tired generation, the American daydream. I loved the way his thin arms swung like loose chains, how his steps were light and quick. While I admired him from afar, he glared at me and proceeded to walk past me like I wasn't even there. Raging, raging hormones. *How do they think with such raging things?*

"Hey guys," Will said apologetically. Will's sweet turquoise eyes trimmed with thick black lashes, squinted innocently, like he could have been the designated driver, but really, he had dedicated the past four months of his life to becoming better acquainted with the worlds tucked into his subconscious. He began eating shrooms with every meal. He called it "menu-dosing." One time, when we were playing The Game, he told me that he liked me because I knew how to swim. Of course, I had no idea what he was talking about because I wasn't a very good swimmer, but he said that it didn't matter. So, I believed him. Giuls was right, he really didn't say much. But when he did, it made it more meaningful. I envied and loved that about him. I think both are possible.

"You guys want a drink?" He asked.

"Did Linda pack any snacks?" Giuls grinned. I shrugged my shoulders.

"Let me go get Ben," Will said, walking off into the crowd. Between the faces, I saw Ben and Ray's mom talking, her shouting something into his ear angrily. It looked like he was trying to calm her down.

"Come on, let's go," Giuls said, pulling my hand through the mob.

\*\*\*

Little blue capsules. "Just take half," Giuls said with waning irises. We found ourselves hovering around the kitchen island with strangers and we stayed there for days laughing and laughing. My head felt like a balloon, tied to the rest of me with swinging ribbon. A boy moved closer to me every time he had the chance. Everything felt so easy and hilarious, everything was *so* funny. He had a sweet, genuine laugh, like his mouth was too small for how funny the joke was. An echo bounced around the chambers. It didn't matter though, I still I wanted to be where Ben was, to fix what was wrong. I was obsessed and I knew it. When I shut my eyes for just a moment, I could feel this pulse in me that felt uneven, unsteady and unhappy without him. *What is wrong with you?* I pleaded with myself.

85

Everything blurred into a hoard of faces and suddenly Ben came storming towards me. His eyes looked grey; no expression formed. I didn't even recognize him at first. He pulled my arm out from underneath me so fast I almost hit my head on the marble-top. He ripped me through the crowd into the backyard. We stood outside in the nippy October air. When I looked down, my wrist lit up red where he had been clenching. The sky was smoky, lit by the moon and car dealership lights that lent to the town. The sound swam back into my ears. I went to put my arms around his waist, but he pinned them back down to my side. I felt like a toddler who kept trying to touch the stove. "Did you smoke out Eric?"

"What? No, whose Eric?" I wrapped my arms around the back of his waist. He let me hold him for a minute and then he swatted my arms away again.

"What the fuck Pais?" Ben said, ripping at his hair. The black pupils of his eyes were so widely dilated I thought, they would explode right there in his sockets. His hands balled into fists. His shirt pocket had a wad of rolled cash into it.

"What?" I said sloppily. "Come on," I laughed and motored my lips. *I don't even know why I'm doing that.*

"It's not funny Paisley," he said. "Is it that you don't like me anymore? You like him, is that it?"

"What? What are you talking about?" I rolled my eyes. "I don't like Eric. I don't even know who Eric is. And you didn't even wanna talk to me. You've been ignoring me all night. And Giuls can't find Will. Where is he?"

"I've been ignoring you all night because I'm. Mad. At. You. Paisley," he said, chopping his hands into the punctuation of each word hovering in the air in yellow subtitles.

My vision violently tumbled down. My chest started to grip at my lungs, like laces being pulled too tight. Then over our heads, a body crashed through the glass doors and the audience cheered. Ben picked a leaf from my hair gently, looked at me with disappointment and walked away.

I walked back into the house, but now I was navigating fields of avalanching paint. Manic smiling faces grabbed at my limbs, moving me like a lead wave. When you're sober, you would call it a panic attack. When you're very much not sober, they call it *bugging out.* The staircase felt like a treadmill pushing me back down. I gripped to the railing when suddenly Kenny rushed by me with another boy. He wouldn't look at me. I went to call for his name, but the sound wouldn't come out.

The bile nipped at my flexing throat. I rushed as quickly as I could for the bathroom door. Ben and Ray stood face to face in the hallway. His face turned to mine - the bricks of the house fell into my throat. I could feel the blue dye burst through the foundation, starting to seep into the wrinkles of my eyes. Too many things happened at once. He stepped towards me and I put my hand over my mouth. I was going to puke. I ran into the bathroom and my guts shot out of my mouth. I felt his hands pull my hair back. "Ben, go away," I mumbled.

"Pais, it's fine," he said rubbing his hand against my back. "Just breathe."

"Ben, go away." My voice radioed back from the ceramic.

"No," he said, his hand brushing loose hairs away from my eyes.

It was the last thing I remembered. Actually, the last thing I remember was Ray laughing, saying that I couldn't handle my liquor. *I'm sixteen, no shit.*

---

The skylight was cruel and insensitive to the changing tides. The sun furnaced into the room, flooding my keyholes. For a moment, I was grateful for the migraine. Everything hurt, like the inside of my skin was sunburnt. A knock came from the door.

"Pais," Chris said with his face creaked through my door. "There's someone here for you."

"Chris?" I said shocked, still half asleep. "When did you get back?"

"Never left kiddo," he half smiled.

"Kiddo?" I grunted, trying to hold my brain in from spilling out of my ears.

Ben sat at the kitchen table with his hands wrapped around a coffee mug. He combed his fingers through his hair nervously. My one eye shut and the other winced in pain. He started to laugh. "How you feeling?"

"I can't feel my face," I groaned. "What happened last night? How did I get home?" I said, shoving my face between my arms. He scratched at the back of my head, running tiny shivers down my skin. *How nice it is to be pet. Maybe I was a cat in another life.*

"Well you threw up a lot and then we walked home and that was pretty much it," he said simply.

"Gross," I muffled.

"Paisley," he said. I groaned at him to stop talking. "Paisley, I'm sorry." I lifted my head and tried to scowl at him.

"No, no, not now," I pleaded. "I think I'm dying. I'm very busy right now."

"No, Paisley. I'm sorry that I was a jerk last night. It's just that you said I wasn't your boyfriend and I freaked out. But if you don't want me then I have to respect that. I fucked up. I'm sorry."

I rolled my eyes and took the coffee from his hands to drink. "For what? For freaking out or for hooking up with Ray?" I shot out.

"I didn't hook up with Ray. We were just talking, and she got a little touchy. It wasn't me. I didn't do anything," he said. "You know I wouldn't do that."

"Oh yeah, I'm sure it was all her... fine, well then then you should know that I do want you and *want* to be with you. I was just fighting with Kenny and I don't even know why I said that. Let's just forget any of it ever happened, ok?"

"Well I don't think that will be a problem with last night," he laughed.

"My brain is falling out of my ears," I groaned and dropped my head to the table again.

It was our first fight and the first time I had seen what Ben was like when he was angry – cowardly and spiteful. It's not that I considered myself mature for my age. In fact, I knew people who felt that way about themselves were usually the opposite. I was as unseasoned as they came. Still, there were so many parts of life *I knew* I was too young to know. So yes, it's naive to say, but it was that morning I realized that Ben wasn't just a daydream. He was real and he had problems and feelings of his own. The loop stopped. Ben wasn't a projection anymore. Even when you're only sixteen, loving someone is a responsibility.

# 9

# Paradise Rockaway

I don't know God the way other people seem to, but sometimes I guess I find myself praying to *something*. That's what makes me think there must be something out there, something fueling the instinct.

If there is a God, I think it's kinder than what Ben thinks about it. He was raised Jewish and he hates God. Saying, "if there is a God, he's a prick." And then he would usually follow up by listing off all of, "humanity's evil apathies." Thousands of starving children, corrupt dictatorships, meat-farms, elephant hunters, meter maids. He had a point.

A lot of people seem to be angry with God, in a way that *it* let each and every one of them down and cut them so deeply that mentioning even the idea of religion is like pouring vinegar into their wounds. They needed God and it abandoned them, dropped them from the sky and let them crash into the bricks of their suburban mansions. I've never been to church, only funerals. I've never been to mass, just heard a Priest mutter prayer over rectangular holes in the ground. I guess I can't say much about it and I'm not sure I have a very strong opinion, but I don't think God has anything to do with our synthetic satires. Aunt Nadine said that God couldn't be found in churches. It was in the tree branches that never tangle, the way our veins look like roots. But she never talked about why the world worked that way and I think people need God for the *why* in their lives. Which might be obvious, I get that. I guess I just wish people needed it for something more important. If you knew why, would that really make it any better?

It was a Sunday morning and the film from my eyes had departed back into my tear ducts. I wondered what happened to all of our atoms when we slept. The way we shed old ones. Do they know they're dying? Little pieces of us always die when we sleep. And it's comforting to know that we are literally always growing anew even in the smallest of ways. Where does all that energy go? Fragments swirling together in a chronic storm, oxygen standing still for a brief moment and the remnants sparkling down into a body's lacunas to form fresh, strong cells.

As I walked down the hallway, I heard the buzz of jazz from the kitchen, the smell of flour and cinnamon. The hallway carpet felt like fresh moss against my tennis socks. Mom was dancing with a cigarette perched into the corner of her mouth, swirling Giuls into her arms. Kenny and Will placed cups and plates down on the kitchen table while Ben and Chris stood over the stove with spatulas in their hands. Mom caught sight of me and excitedly said, "Oh everyone, everyone, she's up!"

All at once everyone turned with smiles plastered to their faces and cheered, "Happy ¼ Birthday!"

Giuls came over and grabbed both of my hands, pulling my limbs to the music. "What's going on in here?" I asked her confused, half smiling, half suspicious.

"Your mom invited us all over for your ¼ Birthday!" Giuls said.

"Because everyone always forgets about your real birthday in this house. It's a family curse," Chris chuckled with charcoal caught in his lungs.

I hadn't spent a birthday with mom in years, but she always sent cards in the mail with cash. Aunt Nadine would make me a cake and I would wish that my mother was there. Tradition.

"Fresh coffee in the pot Pais," Ben grinned at me.

Chris playfully hit Ben on the back of his head and said, "Alright, let's focus on the pancakes. You're letting em' burn."

A peace offering. A ¼ for a 57.11% family. We would spend that morning filling our stomachs with sugary syrup and pancake fluff. Mom bobbed her head up and down with laughter and Chris looked at her lovingly. She was his light; you could see it reflecting off his skin. I wanted to be all of those things to someone, for someone to always come back, no matter what. Is that love? Needing each other? Maybe that's why he came back, because it was his responsibility to. Chris sipped his coffee and I wondered what it was spiked with this time. I wonder if they all knew, if they could smell it on him the way I could. Ben did. He always knew.

The kitchen cleared out. Will and Giuls went back to his family's house for dinner. She made a funny face about it. Kenny went out with a friend from school. Chris passed out on the couch. Mom went outside to smoke a cigarette. Ben and I volunteered to clean up.

"If I had known, I would have gotten you something," Ben said.

93

"It's actually not my ¼ Birthday. I don't think anyways," I tried to do the math. "My birthday is November 11th. Which would make my half-birthday May something... which would make my ¼ Birthday.... I think it passed."

"Hey, at least she's trying," he shrugged, handing me a dish to put into the washer. "And now I can get you a present for your actual birthday." He pressed his lips into mine firmly, nervously. I could tell he felt sorry for me. I hated that feeling, when *you know* someone feels sorry for you. Is there a word for exactly that feeling? The seething, heart sinking anger that occurs when you just *fucking know* someone feels bad for you. "Happy not-birthday," he smiled.

"Thanks," I blushed and turned my face back towards the sink. "Ben, I'm really sorry too, about last week when I said you weren't my boyfriend. I feel weird we never really talked about it."

"That's ok. I've already found a solution." He said, leaning against the counter in mom's rubber yellow gloves. He looked cute, even in plastic.

"Let's hear it," I menaced.

"I'm never gonna be your boyfriend and you're never going to be my girlfriend," he said, screwy. "Because that way we'll never leave... you see that's the trick. I can't leave and you can't leave if there's nothing to leave in the first place."

"So, we'll just be friends forever then and we'll never leave each other, is that it?" I laughed. Ingeniously avoidant.

"That's right, now you're really stuck," he beamed.

"I'm too deep now," I joked.

He kissed my cheek and said, "knee deep, kid."

"Ew. Did you just call me kid?"

"Ok yes, I immediately regretted it. I apologize for ruining that moment. That was my bad. I will take the fall for that... *rambling apology*.

---

There are not enough English words in the dictionary to describe the impossible length of eight hours spent at school. There is no word in existence that defines the way time drags like a net full of rocks being pulled up a mountain. There is no sound to describe the way your stomach backflips, growls from boredom, demands it be removed from the building, tells your brain that you are starving, a hunger pain that could win thespian awards for its fooling performance to trick you into thinking that you hadn't eaten for days. I've never not listened so hard to anything in my entire life the way I've not listened in chemistry class. Sometimes, I looked up and genuinely questioned if the words coming out of my teacher's mouth were in another language. It might as well have been. Why did they force us to fail over and over again at our shortcomings and only brush upon what we excelled at? I should have been homeschooled. We all should have been, right? Doesn't everyone hate high school?

The kid to my left was practically drooling. Then, a thud came from the back door. A piece of loose-leaf stamped "Nurse" stuck to the glass. Giuls, Ben and Will's face moved into the small square window mouthing, *"Go to the nurse."*

I raised my hand and the teacher said, "Miss Ciel, I'm ecstatic you're choosing to participate but questions will need to wait till after the class."

I shot my arm up again and began to annunciate with the uneven power from my chest, "I have my period and I'm profusely bleeding through my pants. I need to go to the bathroom." The rows of harrowing teenagers snapped their heads back. "I need to go to the bathroom because once a month, I shed my uterine lining and-"

"You made your point. Go to the nurse and stay there till the rest of the period," he said angrily.

"Yes, sir," I faked obedience. I held my head high and walked calmly out of the room.

Ben, Giuls, and Will pulled me into the corner to explain the plan. That there was no plan. We were cutting, we would probably get caught, then get detention, and it would be worth it because the ladder was to hover over your body in class like a ghost. So, we ran for it again. Racing down the empty hall, the sounds of our sneakers and faint laughter echoing against the cage. Will, up ahead, whipped back around and all at once, we skid towards the other direction. From behind us someone shouted, "Get back into class!"

"This way, this way!" Will hurried us.

We reached the back staircase, pushed against the heavy double doors and a cold morning gust of air burst through. It tasted like winter and gasoline. The parking lot was plowed with fresh mountains of snow. Winter had barely made a sound when it came in. I couldn't remember it happening so fast.

"Pais, come on!" Ben yelled looking back, with the frost in his eyes. Rows and rows of hand me down vehicles, white stripes against asphalt, the breeze biting at our wrists and ankles. We piled into Will's car and like our little world was being sound tracked, music began to blare from the speakers as we ripped out of the parking lot and onto the quiet suburban trails.

Grey fuzzy fabric on the seats, Ben steaming the dutch in the passenger seat, Giuls breaking up bud on the back-center console, Will handing back a lit joint to me. "Rockaway. We should go to Rockaway," I said, over the music.

"What's that?" Giuls asked.

"It's a beach in Queens."

"Rockaway it is!" Will shouted excitedly. The rush had made his voice higher, his spirit warmer.

The drive was long, but the roads were empty. The car was cloudy, but the sun was shining. We sang along to the songs we knew, which was almost all of them. And that was the moment I realized that we had been listening to the CD over and over again. Giuls' arms swung over Will's seat, hugging him tightly into his chair. He loved her. I hoped she loved him too. I was rooting for them, rooting for the characters in the movies who you believed should have ended up together. Giuls handed me the blunt and without thinking I asked Ben, "Baby, do you want more?"

The three of them turned to me blank faced and silent. "What?" I asked over the music.

"No one make any sudden movements," Giuls said in a bad Australian accent. "This is a rare sighting for this creature"

"Oh, screw you guys," I laughed. "Do you want more or not?"

"Um...yeah, yeah I want more," Ben smirked and opened the car skylight. *It slipped. Baby. Baby. I had never called anyone that before. Baby.*

"No, it's cold," Giuls whined.

"We're about to get off the highway, we gotta air out the car. Take my sweater." Ben said, handing it back to her. Without thinking, I unbuckled myself and crawled through the skylight. The cold hit me like ice, whipping my hair in every direction. "Paisley, make room for me!" Giuls shouted from below. She popped through and screamed, "Holy shit. It's fucking freezing!"

I screamed back over the pummeling wind. Our laughter rocked through our rib cages. We locked our hands together, lifted our arms into the air and howled like fools. The fabric clung to our skin, danced up towards the sky. The hazel in her eyes glistened. I felt Ben's hand steady my legs. He pressed his lips into my side. It was my new favorite moment of us all together. I wish it existed in photos or on video. For a moment, I was filled with fire and I felt red. I didn't know I was capable of changing colors. I always thought I was blue, turns out I'm the hottest part of the flame too.

* * *

We had made it to the shore at Rockaway Beach back in Queens, New York. An unlikely place for grand waters. The four of us sat wedged together on the sand with our hoods over our heads. "It's so cold," Giuls said into my ear, shivering with our arms wrapped around one another.

The wind was harsh, but I felt the sun kiss at my face the way it did on the first day of Summer when I was a little girl. Sometimes I felt her, like she was right next to me. Like instead of leaving, she left a little part of herself for me to hoard and save in the closets of my shelter. And I hope it doesn't leave like the rest of the atoms do when I sleep.

The hours passed and we got so high that I couldn't feel the cold anymore. Ben and I watched as Will threw Giuls over his shoulder and raced towards the water. I sat back on Ben's chest as he tightened his arms around me. He rested his rattling chin atop my head, then nestling his icy cheek against mine. The warmth buzzed between us. We fit nicely together. I told him about Aunt Nadine and the first day of summer. I told him how she died and how I found her, how I could still feel her in my fingertips, the way it got all over my skin and how scared I was to get the blue all over the people I loved. I told him how I hadn't seen much of my mother in almost a decade and how Chris was a drunk. He said he assumed that much about Chris.

For the first time since she left, I felt the bricks she laid into me steady and grounded in my being. The goodness of her, instilled into me was not hidden away like an old sweater but living safely in that wide-open field. Even if the moment was fleeting, already gone, I thought to myself how nice it was to feel so deeply for anything, like I had forgotten how to do it. Sometimes I think if it weren't for Ben and the Inconsolables, I would have never remembered.

*I always thought I was blue, turns out I'm the hottest part of the flame too.*

There are a lot of people out there who have been hurt very badly by God, but for all the millions, Ben still felt like the only person who understood what it had done to me. I'm angry at the way branches never tangle and veins look like roots and the way that Aunt Nadine is gone, and Ben's parents were gone and Giul's father left and Will's family never got closure over his brother's death. And if heaven is supposed to be paradise, then where the hell are we?

"You know when I was little, I really thought Peter Pan was gonna come get me and I was gonna go flying in the clouds," he said, pulling on the joint. I was grateful for his interjection.

"Yeah, me too," I agreed. "I miss it."

"Yeah?" He exhaled. "I think maybe now, the closest I'll ever get was back there, with my lungs on fire and your body out the skylight. You looked like you were flying."

"I felt like a bird," I smiled. "A really pretty one."

"You are a really pretty bird, here on the island of Paradise Rockaway," he joked.

"You're a really pretty bird too."

---

"You can't just cut class because you feel like it!" Mom screamed.

"Ok, I said I'm sorry," I huffed. "I won't do it again."

"Yeah, no shit! And you're, you're grounded! You're super grounded!"

"Ok that seems fair," I agreed begrudgingly.

"That's it? No apologies?" She said, crossing her arms over her chest.

"I cut class once, I said I'm sorry already." I rolled my eyes.

"That's a terrible apology. You know who gives bad apologies? Sociopaths who feel no remorse."

"Ok?" I laughed. I couldn't help it. It was ridiculous and yes, maybe I was still a little high.

"I know life sucks, ok? But you can't just go around cutting class and running around with a boy whenever you feel like it. By the way, who even is this kid? And your school calling, I don't know what to do. They think you've got a serious attitude problem."

"It wasn't just Ben!" I yelled back. "And you met him and invited him over. What, you suddenly don't like him? This is so stupid. I'm going to bed," but what I really planned to do was sneak out and go to Ben's.

"I'm trying here Paisley!" She screamed. "I'm trying to make things better!"

"I don't want you to try," I said, stoic with my eyes stabbing into hers now flooded with tears. "I want her to come back and for you to go away!"

*Where does all that energy go?*

"No, you don't get to say that. She didn't give you back to me! I tried to get you guys back. She took you away so now I'm not going to go away! That's not an option anymore so give me something else here!" She pleaded. "What do you want from me? I'm trying to give it to you Paisley." Her fair flattened out. I hated my name when she said it. I hated that she gave it to me.

"I don't want you."

# 10

# Intermission *

S omething sort of split in me and it let out more than I knew what to do with. It was a physical reaction, but one I could only make sense of by feeling it. I don't know if that makes sense, but sometimes I don't know how to describe what's wrong, but I can see it so clearly. When I think back to the fight with mom, I see a floorboard that's always been loose. Suddenly a person comes running over and the weight unhinges the wooden panel even more. There's just a slight gap, but it's enough for something to crawl out of. *You could fit a handball in there, but nothing wider.* That's what it felt like, like something from the basement of your brain squirmed out from an unkempt ground.

I felt contagious and scared of myself. Scared of who I might bleed into. Scared of what color I was pouring into people when I thought I was loving them.

"It's OK Paisley, don't cry," Kenny said rubbing the burning skin of my back, my curved spine feeling as if it were about to puncture through with each heave. My sobs were so loud I almost didn't realize they had come from my own body. My heart was not an organ, it was a bomb. "She knows you don't mean it. It's OK Paisley. It's gonna be OK."

"But I do mean it. I really mean it. I really, really mean it. I don't want anything anymore. I don't want anything anymore. I don't want anything." The voice went on and on like it was coming from someone else's throat. A rogue string, a sliver of peace that smelled like the ocean, had run a crack through my earth. My brain's flaw had been revealed so *it* decided that we didn't deserve that moment of peace. The tops of the building were falling down from the sky.

"It's gonna be OK... I'm gonna take care of you this time," Kenny whispered. *Please hold me together.*

---

Intermission. I missed school for the next three days. I don't remember much but the feeling of thick fog in my eyes and bricks in my head. I couldn't wake up; I didn't want to speak. I didn't want to see anyone, not even Ben. I couldn't see him like this. I couldn't see a thing at all, just the red mulling through my veins and the bomb in my chest whose fuse I feared would be nursed with too much oxygen, so I took shallow breaths. It was crippling to think about the sun on my skin, so I stayed beneath the covers, beneath the waters. "You're good at swimming," I heard Will in my head. I went back under like I was drowning. *There's an ocean in this bed.* How pathetic am I? I couldn't swim if my life depended on it.

*Please hold me together.*

---

The room filled with light and the sun beat down from the fancy, stupid hole in my ceiling. The air conditioning sounded like a train buzzing in the distance. All I could see was the blind spot behind my eyes and I thought of the trains that passed on the platform in Queens, how they stormed through rusted rails, how all I wanted was to jump... and I didn't. It ripped through the station. My eyes shot open.

I practically hobbled over the patch of carpet I once imagined myself shooting through.

"Chris, help her down the stairs," Mom said.

"I'm ok, I'm ok," I said with Chris's arms guiding me into the kitchen. I sat down at the table and took another deep breath in, feeling my veins inflate with color. The birds chirped so clearly. *Did they always sound so pretty?* I felt my skin against the solid wooden chair, my hands on the cold granite counter, my feet on the still floor. The certain nature of firm furniture felt good and taken for granted. Their eyes bore into me like forks checking to see if the meat had been cooked.

"Can I have coffee?" I asked. They all scrambled at once to the counter.

"Get her coffee, get her coffee," Mom demanded. She wrapped her arms around me and held my trying person, letting my skull rest on her collar bone. "You want milk and sugar?" I nodded. "Get the milk, Chris go get the milk."

"We're out of milk, what-" he panicked.

"Go to the store then Chris," Mom demanded.

---

Mom said it would be good for me to get out of the house. Kenny scoffed that *I would* get out of my first time being grounded. I went to the only place I had to go that wasn't Ben.

Giuls' bedroom walls were lined with posters of all the great female artists: Janis Joplin, Aretha Franklin, Amy Winehouse. From floor to ceiling, vintage queens looked out at us through paper thin eyes. Mine felt like boring craters. Vinyl records, socks and old incense ash covered the floors, wires tangled through sweater sleeves. "Damn, you look like shit," Giuls said, when she saw me.

Giuls explained to me that so much had happened in the three days I had been away. "Will like *really* won't talk to me. I don't know dude. He's just being weird. Like he just won't talk to me the way he used to. Did Ben say anything? She asked lighting a stick of incense on her desk. The patchouli scent warmed my outsides, but I still felt hollowed, scooped out, sort of swishing left and right though I sat completely still.

"No, not about Will," I said. "He's not acting any different or at least I can't tell. I haven't seen him though."

Giuls shrugged her shoulders and sat down at her vanity with three bulbs blown out. "Are you still sick?"

"Huh?" I asked.

"You were out all week. Your brother said you were sick. He texted Ben from your phone," she said, swiping blush over the apples of her cheeks. Giuls always looked stunning, with winged eyeliner, glossed lips and diamond dusted cheekbones. She was beautiful, smart and funny. I felt lucky just to watch her diddle around her makeup drawers, looking for something I never knew the name of. She looked like one of the great women plastered above her bed.

"Oh yeah, period stuff," I lied again and changed the subject. "I like all your posters."

"Oh, my goddesses. They give me strength. They're all the greatest musicians who have ever lived. I'm gonna move to Hollywood next year and find the next great musician of our generation and manage them. I just have a feeling that something is waiting for me out there, you know?" Her eyes beamed with life and color.

"That's so cool, how you just know what you want to do." I exclaimed.

She spoke proudly, her chest puffed. "I've always known. Music is my future. Maybe one day I'll even manage The Inconsolables," she said excitedly. "We would definitely be a punk band. I can totally see it."

"Oh, most definitely punk," I agreed.

"What do you wanna do? You've never talked about it."

"I have no idea," I groaned and threw myself back on to the floor. My eyes locked with Stevie Nick's owl. "I never think about the future. I don't even think about next week. I'm just trying to get through it."

"What do you mean? Don't you know which college you're going to by now?" I shook my head. "Ok, well what about when you were little. Didn't you want to be an astronaut when you were little or something?" She asked, bewildered.

"No. I guess I never thought I could be. I just never thought I would be alive this long."

Giuls laughed again like it was a joke and went back to applying mascara. She thought it was a joke, but there I was, the culprit spewing blue dye all over the room. Maybe if you don't see the colors, they can't get on you or maybe that's when they really make a mess.

"I didn't think I was gonna be alive after my mom found out we cut class," she said, popping our favorite record down onto the turntable. The sticker in the center had sneakers hanging from a window. I watched it start to spin. "You know, she's playing a concert over the holidays at Webster Hall. Wait, we should all go see her!"

# 11

# Cherry Pit

❝ I want to talk," I declared standing in the doorway of Mrs. Skela's office.

For the next fifteen minutes, I paced around the small quarters, from door to window, knee into wooden chair, elbow into filing cabinet and then repeat. She scooped the meat out from her avocado with a cafeteria plastic spoon, looking down at her watch every now and then.

"Anything yet?" She asked beneath her red curls.

"I'm getting to it," I said stretching back the skin at my temples. "I'm almost there. I'm trying to figure out a good place to start so I don't sound like a crazy person."

"Ok, well instead of what you want to talk about, why don't you tell me what made you want to come here?" She tossed the pit into the trash bin.

"I came here because I'm scared," I said, finally sitting down. "I'm scared that all of my friends are going to leave and I'm going to be alone."

"Well everyone - yes, literally everyone else in your graduating class, which is an astounding percentage, will be moving on to college. I know it seems like it's too late, but it's not too late to look into options for you."

"No, no that's not it." I shook my head and jumped back up. "I mean, yes *now* I am scared about that too. But I'm scared about something I said when I realized I was scared about them leaving. I'm an old skyscraper. But everyone is sorta an old ugly building, right? That's what I thought. Like I didn't really understand what people thought about the future. I mean, I knew they did, but I don't know. I'm here and I want to be here, and I don't know what to want next."

"Ok that was a very confusing sentence and I'm not sure I'm understanding what you're saying exactly, but we are making incredible strides here. Keep rolling with it, keep rolling," she encouraged me with a mouth full of avocado. I briefly thought how strange it was to be eating such a soft green vegetable in times like this and why she didn't choose to eat something red all the time for the sake of aesthetic purposes that she clearly took into account in the rest of her life. *Who does that?*

"I'm scared because I said something out loud that I didn't even know my brain was thinking. I said-" Tears started to stream down my face. "I said that I never thought I would be alive this long. I said that out loud. I can't believe I said that out loud!" My teeth stabbed at my inner lip and I struggled to continue. "I didn't even know I was thinking that. I think there might be something wrong with me. But I want to be here. I want to be with my friends and with Kenny. I want things for myself, more for myself. I want to be here."

My legs gave out from beneath me and my body crashed down again into the chair. My face was suddenly between my arms, steaming and leaking like a machine combusting. I felt her arms around me and nails stroke through my hair. "That's good Paisley. That's really, really good. I'm gonna help you stay here. Ok? We're gonna do it together."

---

Mrs. Skela told me that wanting things for yourself was healthy - to focus on hunger instead of apathy - so she sent me home with my remaining options for colleges. Most of them were community colleges, but she said that more and more high school graduates were taking their core classes at affordable schools so they could figure out what they wanted to study or if college was even for them in the first place. The whole avocado thing was a little strange, but I was finally getting used to her bad jokes and annoyingly quirky personality. Maybe a person who helps others for a living really needs to reach in all aspects of their life. She was actually starting to grow on me. Or maybe I grew into her. It's physically taxing to hold someone while they cry, to keep them from falling entirely apart. I knew that the energy I was spilling out was heavy and dark and she didn't have to do that - she didn't have to hold me, but she did it anyways.

---

College brochures and shiny pamphlets covered the kitchen counter. Mom and Chris, both with their reading glasses on, flipped through the pages, reading closely at the fine print which read - pay all of this money and *maybe* your child will get a job one day.

111

"Guys, I'm not even sure I want to go to college." I said.

"Well your guidance counselor gave you all of these options and schools to look into and I think it's a great idea. Chris tell her what a great idea it is!" Mom said, trying to offer him weight.

"This is exciting stuff. Ben, tell her it's exciting!" Chris said, sliding the weight off.

"It's exciting stuff," he mimicked Chris. I groaned and put my face into my hands. "Come on, it's going to be fine. College is cool."

"College is cool," I mimicked him. He threw his arm around me and pressed his lips into my hair. The doorbell rang. "That's Giuls. I'll get it."

"You guys are all going to the sump tonight, huh? Those were some of the days," Chris said longingly.

---

It was the night of the Winter Welcoming Bonfire. Ben kept his hand in mine as we pressed our sneakers down over dead plants, making a path to the flames ahead. The sump's trees had lost all their leaves to the edging winter air. You could see the very ends of the naked branches, and through them, the others trailing down from their yards, like forest creatures hearing a call to gather. In ripped jeans and ratty t-shirts, they raved and howled at what fun it was to be young. Giuls fit under Will's wings, her arms wrapped around his torso. He did seem different when you looked at him long enough. Ben knew something was wrong. He kissed at my forehead, petting my hair, kissing my fingers curled into my palm, doing all of the things you're supposed to do to make someone feel safe and yet I felt even more pathetic than I had before. I wanted to be better. My sentences kept stopping in mid-thought and it was frustrating for me to feel drained of the only voice I could rely on. I wanted to be better, to remember what the hell I was trying to say all the time.

The tribes cheered and the moon seemed to rest right at the center of our world. The "bonfire" was lit in someone's parent's fire-pit they managed to drag into the sump. Everyone's phones were put away, all of us seeming to share a mutual desire to forget the world outside or just make sure we wouldn't have to go sprinting for them tomorrow.

... *and* when the shades of dawn were finally pulled down, I felt the faucet switch on, words scribbling themselves into my tongue again. We were all just so happy, so drunk on cheap handles and so high on Ben's latest strain from *who knows where he got it*. The JV teams stripped down, running around the fire-pit, us cheering them on, the girls holding pom-pom's over their bodies and the boys with nothing but the branded football helmets on their heads. Someone yelled, "Weenie roast," and I just remember it being so funny even though it actually wasn't. Ben made almost five hundred dollars. Everyone wanted more.

Every story from that night would be told differently because that's how our brain's process it. Life is just different for everyone and the sooner it's accepted, well maybe the sooner you can stop giving a damn about another's version. The Winter Welcoming Bonfire would be the night I lost my virginity to Ben Rosen, during the week I decided I wanted to be alive, during the month I drowned in my own bed, and during the year I lost one of the dearest people in my life. Balance. I remember feeling the world balance that night, feeling like I was right where I was supposed to be. I remember it not hurting. I remember not hurting - anywhere.

---

Through everything, Ben still managed to look at me through wonder eyes. With a joint behind his ear, so filled up with smoke and light. Like he had all the life in the world to live, he was just dripping in overtime. Tall as a skyscraper touching watercolor skies with his fingertips, he poured himself into me. The strings of light appeared, synapses branching and building and imprinting our smiling faces and joys to one another's memories. I vowed I would never forget the violet shade of light on Ben's skin that night as we laid in tall grasses. His mouth on me, blossoming through my bones, up to my ears in raging, thunderous, insatiable things. It was so fitting, to leave a part of myself in a place and not in a person. With it, I could finally lay to rest the notion that I was impossible to love and incapable of loving another person.

Or maybe I was trying to make it sound more special than just losing your virginity in a bush in the freezing cold. It was special for me though. Because I loved him with all the working pieces of my heart and all the broken pieces of my brain. Maybe that's love, using what's left of us. TBD.

---

There was a shrill scream, "Cops!" And just like that, the crowd went quiet and began to disperse. Ben, with rosy cheeks, looked lovingly at me and picked out the blade of dry grass from my hair. The flame went out and the embers had been doused with neon jungle juice from the football team's orange coolers now lying empty next to the pit. What a shame, there wouldn't be much left for the morning sprint. Ben said, "they'll make the Freshmen clean it up." Navy sky, maroon and gold pom poms shredded into the grass, the sound of footsteps but only shadows walking off into the distance. "Come on, let's go," Ben said tugging at my arm. "Come on. We gotta go," he urged again.

We rushed out from one of the yards and into the suburban quiet street lit by front porch lights and streetlamps. We shivered in our coats, linked at the arms, my hand safely curled into his again. "You look really pretty right now," he said, Bambi-eyed.

We went back to his empty house. It was always that way for him. Face to face under the shower head, feeling the small rivers melt down, lapping over our skin pressed against one another. His arms were freckled with small beauty marks. I looked up towards him, his head blocking out the rain, and I questioned just exactly how many times a person is allowed to fall in love. It seemed that once would be enough.

"Do you feel better?" He said with his nose to mine.

On the night of the Winter Welcoming Bonfire, three kids in our Senior class were arrested. Will broke up with Giuls and Giuls keyed his car the next morning. His parents caught her on their security camera and wanted to press charges, but Will convinced them not to. While those three kids sat in a police precinct and Giuls' heart broke in two, Ben and I went back to his house, showered, made mac & cheese, smoked, had sex again and fell asleep watching cartoons. When we woke up, there were about a hundred texts from Giuls and my mother asking me where I was. Ben woke up to one single text from Will asking to smoke and one missed call from his Aunt Aggie. She was coming home.

# 12

# Hey, Baby

Aggie was built like a brick duplex. Her lips were lined too far away from her actual shape with a vibrant coral. Her skin was leathered from the sun and her French manicure had yellowed. Her silver hair hung in ringlets around her round face. She wore a turquoise dress with ruffles that flapped when she waddled from side to side. From what I hear, she always wore turquoise. She cursed like a sailor, drank rum when she was back home and drank anything at all when she was aboard a cruise ship.

We sat around the dining room table and she told us how she was raised out in Long Beach near the water and that it's had her heart ever since. When she pickled and shimmied out of her seat for a bathroom break, Rex let me know that she was really raised in Old Westbury too, but at sixteen moved into her boyfriend's parent's home in Long Beach. He said that their grandfather was a mean old man who used to hit her and, "dear old *dead* Dad." Ben laughed and rubbed his thumb over my hand. I didn't think it was very funny, but it wasn't mine to feel anything about. Though I had been in the house almost every day for months, it seemed strange to sit there, like we were stuck in some soap opera on a vintage rounded TV screen. It felt like a fishbowl, the channel left on when everyone was in the other room.

Aunt Aggie walked back in and I noticed she wore puka shell embroidered flip flops. The cracked skin of her feet seemed to be the sound scratching at the floor. It was really just her boyfriend's Pomeranian, digging at the legs of the table.

Three drinks later, Aggie started to make conversation. "Tell me, how did you and Benny meet?" Ben and Rex looked down at their plates, taking a bite of their mashed potatoes almost coordinated like the clips of a music video. "You know his father and I went there too."

"Aunt Aggie," Rex grunted and stabbed his fork into a piece of dried chicken, making a screeching sound when it hit the plate.

"What?" She scoffed. "Oh, for God's sake, it's been years Rex. I think I can tell Benny's girlfriend a nice story without you getting your tighties in a bunch." She took a slug of her drink. Ben took a sip of his wine. It was strange she let us drink alcohol at the table. "Like I was saying, their father, my sweet baby brother, Benjamin Rosen the first, he used to go there. He lived in this house here too. It belonged to my parents, you know?" She waited for me to answer to make sure I was listening.

"No, I didn't know that. That is ve-"

"I can still hear my mother screaming from the basement to throw down the laundry. I think it's haunted by her ghost." I remembered the time Ben and I made out on the dryer. I felt dirty. "Anyways, so Benny dropped out. We all told him not to do it. Worst mistake of his life. That's why it's so important for you kids to stay in school. If it weren't for their mother's father owning a coffee shop, who knows what he would have done. Well him and Ally were always going to end up together, I just don't think anyone knew how literal it would be. Well you can guess how the rest went." She started to laugh, mischievously. Ben never told me his mom's name before.

"Aggie, no one wants to hear that story," Rex shot out, grinding his jaw, hands balled into fists around silverware.

"And you know what, it's ironic they weren't more careful with the bad weather." She stuffed a piece of meat sadly into her mouth.

Rex slammed his empty plate down on the table and stormed off. Ben took another sip from his drink and leaned back into his seat. She was a mean drunk.

"Ah, there he goes!" Aggie shouted from her seat, stuck with her plump sides bursting out from the chair's arms. "Gays are just so sensitive. I know lesbos that could eat him for breakfast. You know if they weren't lesbians obviously." She strangely enunciated the word "lesbian," like it was some foreign word she learned on one of her booze cruises

"I think that went well," Ben smiled. "Anyone want another drink?"

"Always such a good boy Benny," Aggie glared. "I'll take another one."

Ben put his hand on my shoulder and asked, "You need anything."

"No, I'm ok, thank you," I gulped. He kissed the top of my head and walked into the kitchen.

"So, you two do everything together, huh?" Aggie asked suspiciously.

"Not everything," I said, cutting the smiling charade.

"Too much like his father. Always getting into trouble, spending all his time with girls," she shook her head at me.

"He's alone a lot. I think he must like the company," I shot back.

"I'm sure he does." She rolled her eyes at me.

"Cheers to that," Ben said leaning against the doorway. Ben and Aggie raised their drinks to one another in the air and took a swig. It wasn't right but I knew that an understanding was needed in makeshift households. Though I wasn't sure about what theirs was.

---

"That wasn't too bad," Ben said, drying a plate.

"Yeah, I think she likes me," I said sarcastically.

"She doesn't like anyone," he laughed. "She's a narcissist. She never liked me and Rex. She only puts up with us now because we're old enough to take care of ourselves and don't ask her for anything." He frowned and then started to laugh to himself. "When I was little, my dad would take me along with him to visit her. And I would loosen the salt and pepper caps so that when she went to put them on her food, it would all fall out. One time on Hanukkah, I filled her closet up with water balloons. It took me like five hours. My parents grounded me when they found out.

They were so pissed, but after they stopped yelling at me, my dad turned around and winked at me. He was always on my side..."

"You really look that much like him?" I asked. He nodded yes. I handed him a water glass to dry. "And your mom's name was Ally?"

"Yep," he said, kissing my cheek. "Allison Rosen. She was on the morning news." He held his gaze out of the kitchen window.

"Wait..." I thought back to the weather woman on the TV whose voice sounded every morning while we got ready for school. Aunt Nadine would watch the morning news with a cup of black coffee dunking cookies. I only ever listened for the weather.

"Allison Rosen as in the weather woman?" I asked, shocked.

"Yeah, that was her," he said sadly.

"Go where the skies are pretty. That was your mom? I watched her every morning with my Aunt Nadine. That's the only reason she even watched that channel. She loved her."

"Yeah, that was her. Everyone loved her," he said finally. He didn't want to talk about it anymore. We never really talked about it again. He brought memories up here and there, but never anything about the accident. That was off limits.

---

"Wait, he didn't tell you his middle name?" Rex said, pulling at the joint. We all sat on Ben's bed together, watching movies, smoking and eating leftovers.

"Your name is Rex, you can't talk," Ben said, jumping over to him. They wrestled playfully, Ben trying to cover his mouth, Rex holding his arm out to keep the joint from falling.

"Tynan," he shouted out. "Benjamin Tynan Rosen!"

Ben rolled himself off of the bed. I leaned over laughing, taunting him.

"No!" I screamed. Rex wheezed, with tears coming from his laughter.

"It's horrible. Absolutely the worst name in all of history," Rex declared. He took another pull and passed it to Ben climbing back onto the bed. "Isn't it strange how we have these names and we're just supposed to be those people for the rest of our lives? Like before we're even people, someone says, hey you, you little fat nugget, you're going to be a reflection of me and my preferences for the rest of your life. It is absolutely fucked." Rex said "absolutely" a lot and held joints like they held cigarettes in black and white movies. He was *absolutely* a model of elegance.

"It is. Every time I meet someone, I'm going to have to be like, "Hi, my name is pattern." Not that I feel too much like a solid Sara or I don't know Amanda, but what if I did one day? We should be able to choose our own names," I said.

"Yeah, we should. But then again, I would name myself something stupid, like... like um, like Leaf," Ben said.

"I actually think that's a really beautiful name. It matches your eyes too," I mused.

"You think so?" He asked cheerily.

"Definitely. Maybe one day you can choose."

---

Mom picked me up from Ben's house now. She was trying to be a more active parental figure. She said I wasn't allowed to sleepover Ben's house anymore because another mom told her that it was inappropriate behavior and an opportunity for teen sex. She asked me if we had sex. I said yes. She said, "Ok." The next morning, she gave me a box of condoms and said, "you're still not allowed to sleepover." I said, "Ok." And that was that. To be honest, I liked our car rides home. It was a short ride, but I liked to hear her sing along to the radio as she waited for the traffic lights to turn green. I remembered her voice being beautiful. It sounded just like the memories I thought would stay that way forever.

"Hey, baby," she said as I hopped into the car. "How was it?"

I rubbed my hands together for warmth and said honestly, "I think his aunt might be one of the worst people I've ever met in my entire life. Top three for sure."

"Ok, so good," she laughed. "Well, at least you have your *real* birthday tomorrow!"

# 13

# Broken Place *

**B**irthdays are bad luck.

Anything in life that is expected to be perfect, will certainly not be. We were supposed to all go to a concert, but the tracks on the LIRR froze overnight and all the roads were sheeted in black ice. Giuls and Will weren't speaking so it was probably for the better. Ben said that we would have fun anyways.

Mom gave me a hundred bucks and told me not to spend it on bad things. I didn't of course because Ben gave me all the bad things for free. She baked my favorite cake from a box, Kenny ate the frosting off of my slice and Ben had three slices because he was really high. Which was funny at the time, because I was too. Giuls called me and said she would make it up to me.

"How's she doing?" Mom asked sadly.

"She's you know, sad," I said plainly, trying to avoid eye contact dipping my finger into cardboard flavored icing.

"Right, right...we're going to bed. You have till midnight, ok?" Ben and I nodded our heads. "Happy birthday baby," she said kissing my forehead, squeezing me into a hug.

"Night Pais, Happy Birthday," Kenny said running up the stairs. He wasn't Ben's biggest fan. Ben didn't mind it. He would say, "I don't mind," to things like people cutting the lunch line in the cafeteria, Tucker Trigger shorting him cash, the endless carousel of cars and kids on bikes stopping by his house to pick up after school, Aggie talking about his dad, Will and Jess not speaking, detention slips for being late, detention slips for missing detention, Mrs. Skela giving him funny looks in the halls. The things he did mind; people interrupting his train of thought when he was reading a book, when one of his Dad's old records started to warp and skip, losing his favorite lighters, and the morning weather report. That seemed to be it. He would say, "Eh I don't mind. I'm too busy minding you."

We settled into the sunroom when he asked me, "You ready for your birthday present?"

"Ben, you wasted all that money on those concert tickets for us already," I protested.

"Hold on," he skipped out of the room and came back with wrapped gifts

"Thank you, I love it," I said as he placed them down on the carpet.

"You didn't even open them yet," he beamed.

I peeled back the wrapping slowly. It was the vinyl album we had been listening to on repeat in the car and in Linda and at parties. My heart melted to mush. I couldn't think of a better word. Mush. I was mush. I thought of all the times we lay in his unmade bed listening to that record, how whenever "Daydream" came on, my cheeks would blush. My eyes welled up with warm stingy saltwater and I curled into him. "Ah Paisley, don't cry. Come on, there's one more. Open it," he snickered.

The second gift was a record player, a Victrola that looked like the one he had in his room. "Ben. This is too way much."

"Well we couldn't go to the concert so I decided we could just have our own." He grinned widely.

"It's perfect. So perfect. I love it,' I said swiping away a tear. "I love you."

"I love you too Paisley," said the boy with forests in his eyes. We spent the rest of the night fusing our limbs into orange carpet, listening to the same songs over and over again. In a way, it felt like those songs were written about us, every single one, like they belonged to us. They would stay that way even when we didn't belong to each other one day. That record would always play that room, his eyes, birthday cake on paper plates, his smiling face, his hands on my thighs, the snow on the ground, the copper sunrise through glass panels, the sneakers running in circles over and over again. What makes a heart broken is that it feels like it will never stop hurting, what makes a record broken is that it never stops playing.

When Ben finally left (at 6 a.m.), I walked into my room to find a beautiful black leather journal waiting on my bed with a note that said:

*Keep writing it all down. The beautiful, the ugly and the inevitable truths. We owe it to ourselves to look fondly on the past. Show it like it really happened. Especially the good parts.*

*Love, Chris*

---

After my real birthday, things were different. Maybe ¼ birthdays were actually better. The Game had a good run, but it had finally come to an end. Aggie was home, what seemed like indefinitely and Will still wouldn't talk to Giuls. Ben got waitlisted at NYU. He never applied to any other colleges. He said that was it for him. I tried to get him to talk to Mrs. Skela, but he wouldn't budge.

Will wouldn't say why, but he refused to talk to Giuls. Not in an angry way, but in a dodgy way. Just a "no, I'm busy today" and nothing else. I tried to talk to her about it, but she just went on and on about it not being fair and then she would just cry for hours like a broken fountain. I reckoned more of a broken lamp. I came home from school one day and there she was crying and crying to mom about it too. It was like she was drowning in it. Mom poured her hot coco and made her pancakes, the things she *tried* doing to console me, but they actually worked for Giuls. I was glad her efforts weren't wasted somewhere.

Without Will and Giuls, Ben and I found ourselves alone together more, but we didn't seem to talk the way we used to either. And he said he didn't want to talk about it and then got mad at me when I did want to. He was just so irritable, and I didn't want to make him more upset. I asked him once if it was because of me. He started crying and apologized. He said it was Aggie, that she was ruining everything and that he hated her and how he would rather be left alone. "But not from you."

He stopped showing up at the end of my classes. I walked out of history one day and saw him and Ray arguing. I could guess what they were fighting about or what she was fighting for. I couldn't be mad at her though. She loved him. I did too. How could I be mad at her for something I was doing, for something I had done to her first? I knew she hated me, but I didn't hate her. Now him - I could be furious with.

"Hey Pais," Kenny said, walking up to my side.

"Hey," I said, thankful for the interruption, but suspiciously.

"What?" He laughed, grabbing my books from me the way he used to in our old school.

"I thought you were still mad at me."

"Well you know, it's Christmas break so we're stuck with each other. And being mad at you is exhausting. And I miss you I guess," he smirked. "Come on, I'll walk you to your next class."

"I have to make one more stop actually, walk with me to the guidance office."

\*\*\*

"Well don't you look nice," I said, impressed with Mrs. Skela's red dress.

"You know, I'm trying something new out," she giggled and spun around. "This is a nice surprise. You here to see me instead of me forcing you. Who died? Just kidding. Not a funny joke," she scolded herself.

"I got you a little Christmas gift," I said, placing the small red box on her table. Her eyes immediately began to water. She picked the box up and opened it. It was a small enamel pin of a red rose I found at the thrift store with Mom. "It's a small thing but I thought of you and I wanted to say thank you for helping me with college applications and you know, everything else."

"You didn't have to do that. But thank you so much," she said walking out from behind her desk. "I'm gonna hug you now. Do you consent to this form of physical affection?"

"I consent," I said, hugging her back.

"Wait, I have a present for you too." She said excitedly, rummaging through one of her drawers and pulling out an envelope.

"It's a letter from my oldest friend in the world who also happens to be a Professor at Northwestern. I sent her some of your work from your creative writing classes and told her your story. She is a woman who understands what loss can do to a person in their lives, but also how incredibly integral it can become to their creative pursuit. Now it's a real long shot to get into Northwestern, at all, but she has agreed to help mentor you throughout your first year of college so that you can take the necessary steps to transfer to a school with a better writing program for your Sophomore year. Now it is only if you want to of course, but I think you deserved a better shot at this. I know the odds haven't always been tipped in your favor Paisley, but all you need in life is one person who believes in you. Even if sometimes that one person is just yourself."

---

It was time to tip my odds. That day after school, I practically ran to the mini mall in town. Sweaty browed and fists clenching, I marched back into Lohanne's fabric store and said, "I would like a job here."

Yvie, the same woman from my last visit with mom, was standing behind the cash register with a sticker gun. She looked back at me and said, "I remember you. You want some gum?"

"Yes, please thank you," I said with my hand out. She popped a neon green piece in my hand and then waited for me to chew thoroughly through it.

"Ok, come back tomorrow. Wear black pants and black sneakers." She put the pack of gum back into her pocket, smiled and walked away.

"Um thank you!" I shouted after here.

"Paisley?" I turned around and saw that it was Will pushing a cart. "What are you doing here?"

"I wanted a job. What are you doing here?" I said surprised.

"I work here." He pointed to his uniform.

---

It was winter break. Plastic holiday decorations and snow-capped bushes covered the suburban town. The sump was an untouched

Tundra. Aggie was on a ten-day cruise in the Caribbean for Christmas. Rex was home from school, but he was different too, his dark hard eyes riddled with sadness. He would say, "The holidays are just the absolute worst" and "how cliche," of the families that passed by. Mom invited them over to dinner, but they politely passed. When I went over one night, Ben was passed out. I thought he was tired, but Rex said, "he overdoes it on the sleep medicine sometimes." The bottle was nearly empty.

Rex decided that throwing a party was just what him and Ben needed to feel better. Aggie was back tomorrow, and Rex was conveniently going back to the city then too. I tried to tell Ben that it was a bad idea, but he insisted that holidays needed to be redefined with new traditions.

---

There were eight coolers filled with jungle juice and the universe only knew what was in them. I had one cup and the ceiling was on the floor and the staircase was covered in ears. Will was under the hallucination that he was a part of the leather recliner and that the leather recliner was the root connecting humanity to the galaxy. At one-point Ben said, "God, look at all the faces on their boobs." He had imagined that each pair of boobs had a set of eyes where the nipples were. He said they kept staring at him.

I wished Giuls were there, but she was away visiting family with her mom. Ben kept wandering off and leaving me alone. He kept acting all skittish, like I was annoying him, so I sat next to Will who was too high for conversation. I don't remember much besides tripping my face off and seeing Kenny and Rex make out. I think that part was real. At one point, Ben and three velour girls from school stood at the top of the L-staircase and dropped down little toy soldier parachutes, but instead of the soldiers, there were ibuprofen bottles. When they hit the floor, everyone dove like it was candy from a pinata. Instead, small plastic bags of pills and dime bags were stuffed inside. One of the velour girls went to kiss Ben, but he gave her his cheek, stared down at the many eyed boobs on her chest and ran away nervously. Half-naked boys and girls danced on the counters. Silver from my math class slipped off the side and had a massive welt on her face for the next two weeks. Bradley from AP Physics tried to rip his underwear off through his pants, but he failed and after that, anytime anyone saw him at school they would shout, "Take your thong off!" It felt like the world was in fast forward. Fairies twirled about making knots out of the air and our stomachs.

At sunrise, the lot of survivors, about a dozen or so of us, laid outside on the deck. Our breath let out a frosty mist. You could hear the sound of birds chirping and lips smacking together. A hot pink glow rose from the crust of the earth, just high enough above the old wooden fence that we could see it spark like candle flame. *Watch the gap.* The speakers from inside the house were just loud enough to hear the music. *"Will I ever get it back? No, not like that,"* people sang along, sadness caught in their throats.

Ben somehow ended up locking himself in handcuffs and apparently Will flushed the key down the toilet because he said that, "Only the universe should hold the key." I remember Ben replying, "You're so right man." Now he was whining that they were too tight.

It smelt like urine and peppermint. Ben, Will, and I huddled close together for warmth laughing about how screwed Ben was. I don't know why I was laughing. I didn't think it was that funny. I don't remember falling asleep, but when I opened my eyes, Ben was towering above me, nudging me with his foot. "Babe, get up." It was a movie that I remembered in flashes.

"What... shit...." I stuttered, horrified. The house had basically been flipped upside down. Aggie's favorite painting, "A Portrait of Larry the Seagull," had been kicked in. There was toilet paper covering almost every inch of the house and one of the sinks were filled with glass and blood. The couches were flipped over. There was a massive puddle of the red jungle juice that had seeped out from one of the coolers with a bowie knife stabbed through it. Apparently, there were a few other people who had a bone to pick with the merriest time of the year. Ben stood there with broken fluffy pink handcuffs around each wrist and one of the holes in his black jeans ripped all the way down his leg. Half of his face was covered in dirt. It smelled like puke. I smelled like puke. Rex was halfway to Manhattan.

"What are we going to do?" I asked Ben in a panic.

"You should go. Your mom is really mad. She called the house this morning," he said.

---

Ben said Aggie called the cops on him. Rex came to bail him out the next day. I didn't find out about any of it until after. Ben said that he didn't want to get me into more trouble. Also, that it was really the stupid seagull painting that put her over the edge. Mom resorted to house arrest for the rest of winter break. Apparently, another mom told her that was the next step. She was right, I guess. I accepted my punishment. It actually turned out to be fun. Kenny and I took over the living room downstairs that week. We laid out on pillows and watched old Tim Burton films. It felt normal, like it was what teenagers were supposed to be doing instead of finding every possible way to light our lungs on fire.

"So, you and Rex?" I teased Kenny.

"That was a one-time-only never-gonna-happen-again-in-a-million-years kinda thing," Kenny rambled on to his point. "He's like Ben... but gay... aka not my type."

"Why don't you like Ben anyways? He's never done anything to you? I genuinely wanna know. I won't get mad." I turned to him on the couch, my legs tucked into a blanket.

"You're just gonna get mad," Kenny rolled his eyes.

"Kenny, it's me. Talk to me. I wanna know."

"Ben is like... that kid at the party that passes everyone the joint and then asks everyone for money later," Kenny tried to explain.

"You don't like him because he sells weed?" I asked. It was ridiculous for Kenny to think that of him. Ben would never smoke someone out for free and then ask them to pay for it. That was just rude.

"No. I don't know how to explain it. I don't have anything against him, but there's just something off about him. He's nice and stuff and I know you guys love each other but I don't know. It's so intense between you guys. You deserve to be happy Paisley, you know that, right?"

Being grounded just made it more fun. As I crawled out of my bedroom window and onto the garage roof, I wondered how many other sneakers hung from window frames, how many other hands would scrape against shingles, how many other limbs would pounce down into the winter grass as they jumped from leaf filled gutters. How many hollow bodies were pulled across town like a magnet? Because they would do absolutely anything to see and touch the person who made them feel whole or because they *needed* to find themselves in a group of people who felt more like family than the one they were running away from. Jumping down from too high, in that split suspended second, I saw them by the thousands. Loose laces, tumbling hearts, running for it.

Being scared of falling but jumping down despite it, is a quality to be found only in the brave of heart - and ,teenagers.

Being alone with Ben was like Arnold Palmers in the heat, the wind coming through the subway tunnels in the Spring, broken-in denim, frosted beer bottles, sugar caught at the corner of your mouth, dried candle wax on your fingers, grease rainbows in puddles, rolling your "R's", hitting the ball at the perfect center of the racket, waxed floors, new white ankle socks in old converse, the wood of a cherry pit scraping against your tongue, your foot slipping on the bark of a tree and kicking up splinters, the pop of a twisted off cap, just everything that is right and taken for granted in the world. But this time, it felt like I was laying down next to a different person.

We sat on his bed together, tangled as ever, two messes of electrical wires that set off the blender when we blinked. He said his headaches were getting worse. He groaned in frustration and threw a book into the wall, knocking everything from the nightstand. I reflexively recoiled.

"I'm sorry," he said, throwing himself back onto the bed. He looked exhausted.

"It's ok." I crawled onto him, straddling myself over him. I lifted his hands from his face to find him teary eyed and red. I had never seen him so sad, so boyish and lost. I helped in the way I knew how. I put my hands over his eyes. He sobbed into them and I felt his tears trickle down the spaces between my fingers. I let him bleed him into me. I wanted to take the blue away. I thought to myself, how navy I already was, that a little bit more dark blue wouldn't make a difference, but him with all his light and warmth, just that little bit of dark blue would ruin his palette. I didn't know how to make him happy, but I knew what to do when he was sad. *I wanted to take your pain away, but I learned that's not something you can do for anyone but yourself the hard way.* I heard the lyrics in my head, the lesson learned by another, that I should have listened to. I didn't care. I still tried.

When he finally stopped crying, he turned to me and said, "You know I love you, right? That I would never do anything to hurt you?"

"I know that Ben," I assured him.

"Fuck it. I don't need NYU. I can just keep selling and we can go to California or something. We can drive across America like Jack

Kerouac did. And we can just live like that, me selling, and you can keep writing the way he did. We can just do that. We're gonna be OK," he said manically. "We're gonna be ok."

I held him until he fell asleep. I walked home thinking about how for the first time in my life, I was excited for the future, but not the one Ben was talking about. I really did want to go to college and figure out what the hell to do with my life and make Aunt Nadine proud of me. I didn't have the heart to tell him then, that I didn't want the same things as him. I'm not sure I ever did.

# 14

# New Year's Eve *

The snow came in with New Year's Evening. I was on probation, but mom still let Giuls come over. We sat in the living room in our pajamas, sneaking cheap champagne from Mom and Chris. We watched the thousands of people waiting in the freezing cold for the ball to drop in Manhattan. I couldn't believe it had only been four months since we moved from the burroughs. I guess that's what the new year is for, to reflect lovingly on the past, but I couldn't remember the past four months clearly at all. It was moving so fast that I forgot to take better pictures and write it all down. I had decided my New Year's Resolution would be to write at least one thing that happened every day, but of course I forgot the next day.

"You know people have piss bags tied to their legs and shit just so they see the ball drop," Giuls said disgusted.

"People come from all over the world to see it happen. It's special for them," I defended.

"Yeah well I'm glad I'm here," she said shoving popcorn in her mouth. "You know at first I thought that Will and I were gonna get back together like in a week, so I felt bad about keying his car. Then a week passed, and I was like, definitely by Christmas, you know? And then Christmas passed. Nothing. He hasn't said a single word to me. Can you believe that? Now it's New Year's Eve and you know what? Fuck him. Who just decides out of nowhere that you don't love someone anymore? He's just like my dad, but Will is worse because he said he would never do what my dad did. And he did. He just left."

"I'm sorry Giuls." I only said what I knew how to.

"It's fine cause I am never getting back with him. He can grovel and beg, and I will never take his ass back. Never. That's what my mom says. Never go back, because people never change. And she's right," she insisted. Her phone on the coffee table buzzed. We both looked at one another, harboring the same slim hope.

"Oh my god, oh my god, oh my god. No. No. I can't do it. What if it's not him? You need to check it or I'm gonna freak out. I can't do it," she said, throwing the phone at me.

"Ok, I'm gonna check it. If it's not Will, it's going to be ok too. Ok?" I reassured her.

"Ok, ok! Check it!" She squealed with excitement.

I turned her phone screen on, looked up and screamed, "it's him!"

We both squawked at the top of our lungs, cheering and laughing. She dropped to the floor hysterical. "What did he say, what does it say? I knew it, I knew it!" She yelled triumphantly.

Auld Lang Syne started to play from the TV. We jumped into each other's arms again screaming, "Happy New Year!" The ball had dropped. The calendar year was over. Mom and Chris came running into the room cheering with streamers, throwing fistfuls of confetti in the air. How beautiful it should always be.

Sound warps out. *Is this what it's going to be like?* Missing someone, on every important day of your life. On every holiday. On each step forward, there will be a phantom pull on your ankle and a cavern tucked into the corner of the room. I found myself longing for the ancient eggplant colored love seat Aunt Nadine and I watched from last year. She fell asleep ten minutes before she could see what would unbeknownst to her, be her very last New Year's Eve. An un-beginning for an unfinished feeling.

Would I ever forgive myself for not remembering every detail like I should have? I had no hopeful resolution when the night turned into a glossy new year, just a blurry memory.

---

That night Giuls and I snuck out to go meet Ben and Will. By the time we were able to make it out, all the parties were over. Aggie was back so Ben's was off limits. But it didn't matter. All that mattered was that we were together. We decided to brave the cold and meet on the school's football field. Giuls was so nervous, she said she couldn't feel anything, not even the below freezing temperature.

Ben and Will sat on the chrome bleachers, bundled in their puffy winter coats and snow-soaked boots. Stadium lights sparkled behind them. When they saw us, they ran down the bleachers and poured over the bannister cheering, "Happy New Year!"

"Happy New Year!" We yelled back, holding up the rest of the cheap champagne from home.

I ran to Ben and kissed his freezing lips over and over until the ice melted. He cheered again, trying to spin me, hardly being able to lift me from the ground before slipping on ice, bringing us both down. Our lungs filled back up with laughter.

Just a few months ago, triathletes moving on to colleges with full rides and impeccable school records raced across the lawn. Now it was covered with snow and four fools with numb fingertips and racing hearts. We were all finally together again. We stood with our feet planted into the snow, counting backwards from three (always) and popping the bottle of champagne open into the obscurity of a new lifetime awaiting.

I literally couldn't feel my fingers or toes and I truly, honestly didn't care. We sat down on the aluminum steps and played the game for the very last round. It was our way of ending things the right way. It had only been a short time all together, but just like that first time we sat in Ben's living room; we knew exactly how special it was to have each other. Maybe we were all insufferably inconsolable in our own ways, but we were all messed up together. Again, and again, until all of our bottles had run out, we toasted to what we considered to be the greatest game that ever was. Quietly, I toasted to the unfinished feeling, the most memorable year of my youth, and the peculiar patterns all the broken glass made from the blown-in windows.

When the night was over, we did what we always did. We paired off. Only this time, Giuls and I walked back to my house. She cried and cried, and the tears almost froze there on her cheeks. "It's really over," she whimpered. I squeezed her hand tightly and told her that everything was going to be ok. She said that she knew things were better this way. While we waited for her mom to pick her up, she said, "Will isn't like my dad. He's good. He was really a good boyfriend. I think that's why this hurts more. He said, "you can't lose someone who isn't going anywhere." So, I guess in a really lame way, he kept his promise."

*-the peculiar patterns all the broken glass made from the blown-in windows.*

---

*Giuls 1/01/ 2007*

I can hear her crying through the wall again. I don't know how many more nights I can do this. God, I wish she would just stop crying. If I could just get one night of sleep, just one night. No matter what I do, I can't sleep. I try to turn the volume all the way up in my headphones, but it's never loud enough. Thank fucking god, the holidays are over. Maybe the bad part is over. Why doesn't it feel that way?

"Just fucking say it, Will! Just say it!"

"I can't be with you!"

I know she still misses him. I can hear it. I can hear it through the wall. No matter how many times she says he can go rot with his skank, disgusting new girlfriend, I can still hear her crying through the fucking wall about it. And I'm the one who can't sleep. Why does it feel so much louder tonight? I've told him straight to his face, that she's a mess without him, that he's ruining our lives - that he's ruining *my* life. He doesn't care. All he says is that "he can't." Bullshit. I hate him. Well, he can go ahead and start a new life and spend all his stupid holidays with his new stupid girlfriend, but I will never speak to him again. I don't care how many times he calls or texts me or sends money. I will never speak to him again. You can't just hurt my mother, leave me to take care of her and expect me to still be there. I hate him. I don't need him and I don't need Will.

"Of course, I still love you, Giuls."

"So, what you just don't need me anymore, is that it?"

"No, no. That will never be it. I still need you in my life. I know it doesn't make sense right now and I wish I could explain more, but I can't stay."

"Please stay."

Is everyone going to leave? Is this how life works? I know I sound dramatic, that I'll look back one day and think of how stupid and young I am, but right now it hurts so badly. It feels like it's never going to stop hurting, like I'm going to crack in half and be broken forever. The idea of feeling this way forever, it's fucking killing me. It's killing me. I can't breathe. Why is it so loud tonight?

"Are you kidding me? You're breaking up with me? You're the one who wanted to be with me!"

"Well, if you didn't want to be with me, then that should make it easier, right?"

"You know what? You're right. This makes it so much easier. You're so right because you're so smart and you're always right, Will! You're right! This makes so much sense!"

"I'm sorry I said that, ok? I'm sorry, but it doesn't change anything."

"But what doesn't it change? Is it me? Do I need to change? Is it me? Please, just talk to me. Just stay and talk to me."

"I can't, I can't. I'm sorry."

"Please stay."

I can't sleep. I can't sleep because every time I close my eyes, I see *him* walking away and pounding her fists against the door and dropping down to the floor. I hear her crying and I can't stop myself from crying. I can't sleep because I can still feel *him* slipping through my fingers. I can remember the first night in the cherry pits together and how it smelled like beer and how I realized how much I loved him because I trusted him. I thought that was love, trusting someone to never hurt you. I thought loving someone meant never being able to hurt them. If it's true - I can't handle what it means. That would mean they never loved me. That can't be true.

On this New Year's Eve, I learned that someone can love you and still leave.

# 15

# Love Yourself More

**T**he haze of dopamine finally started to settle and I could feel myself coming through the milky fog. I felt good, really good. Everything at home was oddly calm. I was starting to put money away in my college fund from a part-time job I actually liked. The Inconsolables were back together again. Will and Giuls were back to being friends. We all hung out after school and went to parties and smoked a lot more than we should have, but things were better.

It was still different for Ben though. With Aggie back and me having a job, we didn't spend as much time together and I tricked myself into thinking he was doing alright with everything, but I was wrong. He would never say, but a part of me knew I was ignoring what he was going through. I was so caught up in the feeling that I could breathe again, free from the weight on my chest. Why does feeling happy seem to always come with a consequence? Life can be so stubborn about weighing the scales out. *Karmic debt collector.*

I woke up one morning to about thirty texts and missed calls from Ben. He wouldn't answer when I rung back. When I went outside and he wasn't there to walk to school together, a guttural twist tore at me. I ran as fast as I could through the sump to his house. I drummed on the front door until Aggie finally answered.

"What are you doing? It's seven in the morning!" She scolded me.

"I'm sorry, I'm sorry," I shot past her and ran towards Ben's bedroom. My blood was rushing with adrenaline, my limbs charged with muscle memory. I swung the door open and Ben was just lying in bed. I shook him awake in a panic. "Ben, Ben wake up!"

He jumped up instantly. "Paisley...what is it?" He said groggily.

"Holy shit," I sighed in relief. "I got a million missed calls from you and then you didn't answer, and you weren't here this morning again. I got scared!"

"I'm fine, I'm fine," he said, hooking me into the covers. I felt his breath on the back of my neck and sighed in relief. He squeezed me into his chest. I heard the ominous crackle of the end grain on the finished record spinning and spinning. Through all the running and smoke and snow, that was the moment I accepted something was wrong.

Since we were already twenty minutes late, we took our time walking to school. He kept teasing about the way I barged past Aggie, but he never did say why he called all those times. When I asked him, he lied about it. I didn't push. I didn't want to force him to do anything that made him feel sad. I gripped his hand in mine and when I pulled it up to kiss it, I saw his knuckles tattered. "What happened?" I asked shocked.

"It's nothing." He pulled his hand away from me. He lied again.

\*\*\*

After school that day, Will and I were at work pricing out fabrics at the cutting counter. When I told Giuls about Will working there, she was shocked. Apparently, Will's family was one of the wealthiest in town. She couldn't understand why he needed the money. It didn't take long for me to figure out that it wasn't about the money for Will - it was about the quiet. Lohanne's never had more than a dozen people in it, customers and employees included. He was more of a wallflower type than he let on. I wasn't exactly a television personality either. The quiet was comfortable. It felt nice to not have to try so hard for once to fill the air.

"Hey Paisley, I want to ask you something?" He carefully laid out a rose-pink silk layer of fabric on the counter.

"What's up?" I said handing him the shearing scissors.

"Do you think it's possible to love someone, but not want to be with them?"

"What do you mean? I need more context," I pushed him for details. I knew I would have to relay this kind of information back to Giuls. I made a mental note to ask good questions.

"Giuls and Weston, my brother who died when he was a senior ... I found out that they hooked up when she was a freshman. At first, I was fine. It was a long time ago and it's a small town. I'm not mad at her for it. I just… now, I can't *be* with her, be with her without seeing… It's like he's standing there when she is. Is this weird for you? I don't mean to put you in that position, but I figured with your Aunt, you know, you would get it."

"No, no it's ok," I said, leaning against the counter. He swiftly moved the scissors down the fabric ruler as tiny threads came loose from the near perfect trim.

"I'm sorry," he apologized. I didn't understand why he chose me instead of Ben to talk about it with. Out of us all, out of really anyone I knew, Ben endured the most loss. Not that loss is quantifiable, but somehow it feels like you still count misfortunes up in your brain. Maybe Ben already knew, and he had lied about not knowing too. "I love her. I just can't, you know?" He looked over sadly one last time before walking off. He left the silk fabric split in two pieces on the counter.

Will must have left early because I didn't see him for the rest of the night. I felt terrible that I wasn't able to console him, but I just didn't know what to say. They always tell you in movies and in books that loving someone means staying and coming back for them against impossible wars raged against you. In wedding vows, it's until death do you part. No one ever talks about a time to leave, just that not you're supposed to do it if you really love someone.

It was closing time and I was on flower aisle duty. It was my favorite actually. There was something nice about the way plastic flowers never withered away. "You want gum?" Yvie asked me, rolling a cart into the aisle.

"No, I'm ok, thanks." I declined politely and placed an orchid in its proper bundle.

"What's wrong witchu?" She rolled slowly in with both feet up on the metal beam, like a kid at a grocery store.

"Can you love someone, but not want to be with them?" I asked.

With a memory flickering in her eyes, after careful thought, she finally said, "I think if you love yourself more than someone you love... you know when it's time to go."

---

That night in bed, I couldn't stop thinking about what Yvie said about loving yourself. She was speaking from her own experiences. I imagined her face aging backwards, the wrinkles smoothing out, her cheeks filing back up with color, her silver hair bouncing out into dark chocolate curls. Forward and back, forward and back. Her memories, as clear as the reel reflecting in her eyes. It's hard to imagine Yvie in love, blushing crimson and diamonds dancing in her eyes. It's hard to imagine myself like that, but I guess I never really thought about myself very much. How nice it is to get lost in another.

I spent so much time wondering what love meant between people that I never considered how I felt about myself. Learning to love yourself is a lesson you learn from loving others. How you love inward is learned. Maybe Will was learning to love himself more.

The next day at work, I found Will in the supply room with a bundle of artificial sunflowers in his arms. "Oh, hey Paisley," he said through the petals.

---

The only letters I received from the seven colleges I applied to were rejection letters and one waitlist from Queens College. Mom hung it on the fridge, saying it was the closest anyone in our family got to college and "trying even despite failure was motivation to keep trying harder." Her AA sponsor told her that. I wondered if I would ever meet them. Kenny saw it, he laughed and drew a penis on it. "Very mature Kenneth!" Mom yelled at him.

---

"Your mom is right! Most of these colleges have already accepted students. It's not going to be easy to get in this late in the game," Mrs. Skela exclaimed.

"I know. I'm just scared that it means I won't get in anywhere at all."

"I'm gonna let you in on a little secret Paisley. I don't know if you noticed, but I always wear red," she said, like she was confessing some big secret. She wore red so much, kids at school started referring to her as a stop sign. "I used to tell people I did it because I was colorblind, and it was the only color I could make sense of. That was a lie though, in a way. I wear red so that I don't feel blue. I'm taking my happiness into my own hands. Sometimes you can't get all the sad out, but that doesn't mean that you have to let it define you."

"Are you saying that I shouldn't let my rejection letters define me?" I asked, sarcasm om my tongue.

"Yes, I am, but I'm also saying that when bad things happen, you have to do whatever you are humanly capable of to push past them. You must always, always be red."

# 16

# A Tangible Reverie

**W**inter usually dragged on in Queens for an eternity with the mounds of hardened snow piled up against street signs and abandoned cars with windshields full of orange tickets. Somehow in the Suburbs, it was already February and we all felt time slipping away faster than we could wrap our heads around. It was Valentine's Day and Ben insisted that we all spend it together. He even got permission from all of our parents to take the day off from school. We thought he was joking when he said it, but he told us that he wheeled the dead parent's anniversary card. No one laughed, but him.

It was so unlike Ben to get all worked up over a holiday, but he just kept insisting that it was worth celebrating. All of our parents dropped us off at the Long Island Railroad station in the town over. He threw his arms into the air and revealed we were going into the city. "Well yeah, duh," Giuls said waving at the train station. I was excited, I did my best thinking on trains.

I worried today would be hard for Giuls. She still talked about how much she missed Will. She said she could feel him falling back into all their old patterns, like laughing over inside jokes or splitting sandwiches at lunch. She talked about how she missed him the most when she least expected it, like when she went for a jog and almost ran into a car in the dark. It was his job to watch out for cars. She said, "See I miss him so much, it's almost killed me." Poetic. Each time, I came close to telling her about Will seeing Weston's ghost, but I could never bring myself to it.

One day her mother was going through old photographs of their golden retriever who passed away and Giuls cruelly said, "You're a divorced fifty-year-old woman. You don't need another dog. Besides, you can't let ghosts keep you from living your life. What you need is to get out of the house and stop crying about your dead dog and asshole ex-husband." Her mother burst out into tears. The next day, Giuls was forced to clean out the attic as punishment. And, she got a new dog.

Maybe it's because of the way I used to stare so intently at them together, how thrilled he used to seem making her laugh or the way his feet used to point to wherever she stood in the room. It seemed so clear to me how far Giuls had to reach for any sliver of affection from him now. It looked like it physically pained him to be near her, but maybe he decided to be friends with her because he didn't want to be like her dad.

Ben stared through the train window. A vision came to mind; him sitting in a massive college classroom, running through the halls with his hip friends in muddy boots trailing behind him. I saw him rolling out of his dorm bunk hungover and storming through a sea of citizens with his textbook hooked in his arm and the cold air pushing the collar of his shirt backwards. I didn't see myself in it.

When we finally reached our destination, Ben led us into Central park and lined us up underneath a small bridge. The air was perfect. The snow was melting, but still covered the grass and tops of the boulders.

"Ok guys. Close your eyes and put out your hands." He pressed his lips to mine, whispered into my ear, "Happy Valentine's Day" and placed one object in my right hand and a small box in the left. "Alright. Open them."

"Hell yeah," Will exclaimed.

"Shrooms and chocolate?" Giuls asked, shivering in place.

"That's one half of the surprise. You'll get the other once we get inside," he said, excitedly pointing to the Museum of Natural History across the street. Eating the shrooms with chocolate was festive and it also took away the gross taste and gritty texture. Maybe I should have been more hesitant, but I chucked them into my mouth. Again, I was excited. I had only been to the museum on school trips when I was younger, but I remembered hating the long ride on the yellow bus and smell of the gift shop. I used the money Aunt Nadine gave me to buy a candy rock lollipop that I never ate because I thought it was too pretty. It melted during the summer.

We followed him blindly through security, down the halls and past exhibits until we finally made it to the Planetarium. Ben's jaw hung in anticipation, waiting for us to put the pieces together. Giuls was the first to understand and started to slow clap. Ben pulled out the tickets to the first Planetarium showing and fanned them towards us. We broke out into laughter completely astounded at the scam Ben had managed to pull. He was a genius. Not only had he convinced all of our parents and teachers to let us go to the museum, he got us out of a science assignment, *and* planned a field trip to Mars.

\*\*\*

My body melted into a soft chair that felt like a bed of moss. Our four pairs of headphones were connected by a single splitter that Ben bought the week before. He thought of absolutely every little detail. We all sat clinging to one another's arms like we were on a ride at an amusement park. Thousands of little twinkly stars shot out above us, the Milky Way painted close enough to touch. *"All the gardens are gone, I've hid them under your tongue."* The words swam through our ears like the milky way - ears flooding like our chairs dropped into a pool. It was stunning, a fragment of reality that he had bent into another plain of existence. A tangible reverie. We were amongst the stars, close enough that we could feel the heat sizzle off them. We were the colors that didn't exist. A portal to another dimension. Dragon skies. Wonder eyes. This was Ben's way of telling us how much he loved us. It was my favorite memory of us all together and it's the one I prayed to Orpheus clouds to hold and write histories for.

---

"There are a hundred billion stars in the milky way, that's about as many neurons as there are in our brains," Ben said to us, on the train ride home.

"Hm," Giuls sounded, thoughtfully. The rest of us nodded in accord.

"Can I open it now?" I asked Ben, pulling out the small box he tucked into my hand in Central Park. He nodded and laid his head

153

on my shoulder, still coming down. He ran his hand over my leg and I carefully slipped the ribbon off. It was a thin gold chain with a single pearl in the center. "It's so beautiful, Ben. You didn't have to do that, but I do love it so much."

The card read, "my sky, my pearl lining."

I started to cry. He laughed, holding my face in the palm of his hands. "Cause you told me that one time that your Aunt Nadine told you that your last name means sky in French." I let out a wail and embarrassingly sobbed there in the palms of his hands. "Oh no, no, don't cry, baby. It's supposed to make you happy."

"I am happy," I cried again, unsure of what I was feeling. "Do you mean that? That I'm your pearl lining?"

"Yeah, I do. You're the only thing that makes me happy anymore Paisley."

It absolutely struck me down how I had somehow managed to be someone else's source of light and happiness in the world when I could barely muster up those feelings within myself. I wondered what Ben really saw when he looked at me because when I looked at me... I didn't feel the same way he did. I felt like the swelling storm cloud, not the sky.

---

"Fuck off!" Rex screamed down the grey carpeted stairs. The stairs that absorbed blood and beer and spit and still managed to stay the same obscure, gloomy tint of dust and grime.

"Get your goddamn ungrateful ass down here right now. We're going to go visit your father's grave!" Aggie hacked into her sleeve. Her skin looked particularly leathered, *absolutely* parched today.

Ben stood in the doorway, playing with the hole in his Ben's Eagle shirt, poking his fingers through. Aggie's foot tapped on the tile, her toes curling over the edge. It was technically still winter, but that didn't stop her from flapping and squeaking her sandals back and forth. The floor screamed beneath her feet. Sometimes if I stared hard enough, really long and good, the white saliva would garner around the corners of her mouth like the acid in batteries in old remote controls. "Ah, come on Aggie, he doesn't want to go," Ben groaned. "Let him be."

Aggie screamed like the whistle on a freight train, "I'm giving you ten seconds or you're not going to have a co-sign on your financial aid! Do you hear me?" Ben's parents had life insurance, but their will had specifically stated that they wouldn't see a cent until they both graduated college. Rex needed Aggie's signature for financial aid, and she threw it in his face every time she got the chance. Three minutes later, we heard the thud of slamming wooden armoire drawers and an exasperated huff. Rex shuffled down the stairs with his frown drooping to his shoulders. "You know if it weren't for that twatty attitude of yours, you would never know you were as gay as Elton John," Aggie said. "You stomp around like a damn drag queen."

"Alright kids, let's all play nice." Ben swung his arm over my shoulders and kissed my temple. He didn't mind. Aggie pretended to gag and that made Rex smirk. But only for a second and then you could see his brow contort with hurt again.

Ben drove us all down to Plain Lawn Cemetery. The last time I was in a cemetery was for Aunt Nadine's funeral and to be honest I don't remember much of it, just that when I looked down at my shoes in the grass, I felt as if my own legs weren't attached to the rest of me. I dreaded the idea of going back, but Ben asked me to, and it wasn't a surprise that by that point I would have done just about anything to make him happy - even if it meant another hundred nights of layering fallen bricks onto the walls.

Valentine's Day was the last time I saw him really smile and it was just because he was high as hell. I missed having an effect on him. Sometimes, it felt like he forgot I was even in the same room as him. I knew he still loved me because he told me all the time, but his "I love you" was starting to sound like an "I'm sorry." I couldn't figure why.

Tombstones were dated as far back to the 1800's. I tried to focus on the numbers and which era they belonged to, on the disintegrated thousands dollar, silk lined coffins instead of what was inside of them. Dead flower heads blew across our steps as we walked. Cemeteries exist only in a perpetual Spring and its trouble with letting go. I used to think it was an outdated ritual to put people into the ground, like some kind of spell we tried to cast to keep them on earth. When Aunt Nadine died, I learned that tradition is important in times of tragedy because it tells us what to do next. The tradition of funerals and cemeteries and flowers on graves are simply steps you take when you decide to keep going. I remember the way Mom sat at the kitchen table for hours making calls to Aunt Nadine's friends in her book club and distant relatives and writing down funeral home quotes and working out times and finances. I was jealous of the way she was able to work out what to do next when I was at a complete loss for how I would move forward in a body I was floating above.

I think more people believe in ghosts than they do in gods. People might pray to gods, but they beg ghosts - to come back, to show them a sign, to take us with them. Do the dead think about the living the way the living think about the dead? Do they find us silly, praying and willing a heart to pump again? Do they wish we would just let them rest in peace so they would stop having to live up to our memories? Purgatory is a word for the in-between, an infinite sameness. In movies, it's a white room. I always thought of it as a dentist's office. Maybe our memories are what keep our loved ones in purgatory because they're always being called back to act our dreams and skewed delusions. When I dream of my father, his face is just a blur and he's always just kinda ... standing there. Maybe he's not in the gap, I am. Last train blown past. A tangible purgatory.

I hope when I go, I don't take parts of people with me. The world is already so heavy, without our full hearts to hold us down, we could just float away.

Ben said Aggie was religious about visiting her brother. We stood around the joint grave. Rex's face was beat red, glimmering from a stream of tears, his forearms holding in his guts. Aggie left a small bottle of rum on top of the tomb. Ben choked on the ice in his chest. No flowers, no nice words, just a simple "what you do next."

*Allison and Benjamin "Benny" Rosen, beloved parents, family and friends.*

Ben reached for my hand and I held on as tight as I could. If you hold something broken together just right, the cracks are almost undetectable, but once you let go, the pieces fall apart again. Every time I let go of Ben, I knew where it left him, back in broken pieces. Our feet were planted side by side in perfect green grass nourished with ashes and leaked saltwater. I imagined decrepit hands shooting up from the patches of dirt where Aggie stood, clawing at her ankles, their gnawed fingertips slipping on all of that sun tanning oil and rum seeping from her skin. I wished she would just go away, back on one of her cruises. None of us wanted to be here. She just didn't have the guts to go alone. She said later, to Ben, "let this be a reminder." I wanted to punch her in the face. *Why would you say that to him you cold-hearted treacherous human?*

Ben shook at my hand and pointed to a bushel of dainty, powder blue flowers. "Those are called Blue Star Creeper."

"Sounds like a cool band name," I remarked.

"Well they're poisonous if you eat them." He shrugged.

"Why would you eat them?" I asked.

"I don't know. I just think it's funny they're growing in a cemetery. Maybe this whole place is poisonous."

*don't cry, baby.*

# 17

# Rust

I t happened again. I knew it would. Like I said though, I would have done just about anything to make Ben happy. And I knew that meant another hundred nights of layering bricks. The power surged; the lights went out. The fire escapes and their rods melted. No way down. The foundation rocked and cracks ran through the cement. The windows blew in and glass covered the floors. I stood still and helpless to a force of chemical nature that brought my building down. I knew it would.

Kenny stayed home from school to take care of me. He said, "everyone gets sick sometimes."

"Not like this Kenny. Something is wrong," I cried. He pet my hair and told me everything would get better. He looked at me like I was defected and dying. Truthfully, I felt like I was. It started just like last time. One second I was crying about something stupid and the next I felt like I was having a heart attack. "I don't understand what's wrong with me. It didn't used to be like this," I cried into his arms. I leaked and leaked my dyes into his cloth, and he held me tightly despite it.

"There's nothing wrong with you Paisley. Our brains get sick sometimes, that's all. You're different, not wrong. It just takes some getting used to."

"What takes some getting used to? What's wrong with me?" I asked him.

My whimpers turned into heaves. I was drowning in the dye. My blood ran royal blue all the way up to the sclera's of my eyes and I saw nothing but a world in a hue of dejection. It left me mangled, dizzy and helpless. I couldn't explain what I was feeling because there was a numbness drilled so deeply into me that I almost felt like it wasn't me in the hollow body. What do you call that? How do you say those things without sounding like a crazy person? It was like trying to use concrete words to draw an abstract painting.

That night I heard Kenny and Mom talking outside of my bedroom door in the hall. They must have thought I was asleep, but most of the time when my eyes were closed, I was just under a wave. "She's sick." Kenny said, firmly.

"Well what do I do?" Mom's voice stuttered nervously.

"I don't know. You're the parent. You're supposed to know what to do," Kenny said angrily.

---

The next day Mom decided that I would see a doctor, but the doctor said that I was physically fine. Instead, she recommended a therapist and wrote us a referral for a doctor who typically worked with teens. She smiled kindly and said, "It's most likely that you're suffering from panic attacks. It's a very common occurrence. Of course, I can't say for sure, though I can say physically, everything looks normal. You're going to be just fine."

On the highway, I counted the white lines the car rolled over. Mom turned down the radio and finally asked. "So, what do you think baby?" Her fingers curled tighter around the steering wheel.

"Aren't therapists expensive?" I said, looking out the window. The droplets of rain appeared on the glass.

"I wouldn't know. I've never been to one," she said.

"What about when Dad died? What did you do?" I knew the answer, but I wanted to hear her say it out loud. Maybe I didn't think she would have the courage. I was being cruel by taunting her and I didn't know why.

"I lost my fucking mind," she laughed. "I should have seen a therapist, but I didn't have anyone to tell me what to do or to take care of me. But you do, so I think you should go."

---

*Maybe I can fix it on my own. If I write it down, not the good parts, but the parts I never think to write down. Maybe I just need to get them out of me.*

*I feel useless. I feel incapable. Like I'm floating and drowning at the same time. Like the song, "I know how to fly and I know how to sink. But nothing in between." Where do I exist? Is it like this forever?*

*An eternal blue desert and tundra and rainforest and city under the ocean. Mountains that stretch farther than the eye can see, a sane mind could fathom. Every land and depth covered in a pale, nightly glow. Nothing, but vast land, blue hills for kilometers. I'm under the ocean, kicking and kicking my feet through the heavy seas, reaching for the thin film where the water meets the sky. At night the silver rivers leak from my eyes, into my throat, and seep through my system. I feel the cartilage in my spine oxidizing, leaving rust in the gaps of my vertebrae and it makes my body ache when I move. I let out creaks and when I try to catch my breath it feels like a freight train storming over gravel. I spit sparks and pieces of myself that are no good anymore. The dead cells aren't leaving, they're stuck to my skin. When the sun comes through each morning, I rot all over again.*

*I don't know how much longer I can do this. There's too much of it this time. I feel sick and foggy. Like the static from a radio. I exist in the grain. Humming through my head. Repeat it again and again until I believe it. The lyrics are a bible. A bible as in a book people need to keep going, to find a reason, to carry through even when they don't want to. I drop the pin on the record like I can see the words on the black rings. She sings. The inevitable truth. There will always be someone that you miss that's left a hole in you. I always thought I was blue. I'm building you up. Turns out, I'm the hottest part of the flame too.*

---

"Alright, what's wrong? Why aren't you talking?" Mrs. Skela asked, impatiently. "Did you and Ben have a fight or something? Let's get into it so we can get to the college business."

"There is no college business. I didn't get in anywhere and I'm not going to get in because I'm not smart enough. I appreciate everything you've done for me, but I can't do this anymore. I thought I was getting better, but I'm not better," I spat venomously. The idea of applying to more colleges and writing another stupid essay about what made me worth taking a chance on, was asphyxiating. I knew the truth about who I really was - inconsolable and unfixable.

"Who said anything about better? We're not up to that part yet."

"What do you mean?" I asked puzzled.

Mrs. Skela's usual warm expression, went cold. She shouted, "God, line! Can someone give this girl a script? I'm sick of working with amateurs! Call my agent, somebody call Barry!" Mrs. Skela shouted. The stage lights flashed on. The fourth wall disappeared. Camera stops rolling.

Neck snaps up to bell. Wooden desk dream. Drool on wrist. School lets out. We're not up to that part yet. *Yeah, you. The you, reading this. I said we're not up to that part yet. What, you thought getting better was going to happen that fast? Get a grip.*

---

Ben didn't go to school again. He was never there when I needed him anymore. He skipped at least once a week now and he never said why, only that he didn't feel like going. I walked over to his house after school. I was down the block when I saw Ray's car pulling out of the driveway.

Normally I would just ignore Ray, but my head tumbled into a rage. Next thing I knew, I was tearing through the front lawns, stepping over icy patches of grass and banging on Ben's door like a crazy person again. He swung the door open shocked, "Paisley, what's wrong?" I stormed through. "What's wrong?"

"Is that why you've been acting so weird lately? Are you kidding me? With Ray!" I screamed. I began to pace in circles.

"Paisley calm down. She was just picking up from me. Paisley!" Ben pleaded with me, trying to turn me towards him.

"Fine, but don't touch me!" I shouted in his face.

"Paisley, nothing happened. Please just stop," he said, calmly.

"Then why have you been acting so weird lately? You lied about your hand. And about Will. How do I know you're not lying now?" I cried.

"You lied to me too. I know you weren't sick last week!" He shot back at me.

"Yes, I was! That's not lying. That doesn't count!"

"Oh yeah, then what were you sick with? Paisley? Why can't you tell me?"

"I don't know what's wrong with me!"

Aggie came from down the stairs and yelled, "Shut the hell up, I'm sleeping. If you can't be quiet, then get out of my house!"

It was three in the afternoon.

* * *

Ben and I sat face to face on the edge of the bed together. Stuffy nosed and steaming from shame, I looked desperately around the room for something other than him. He held my hand in both of his, rubbing his thumbs lightly into my skin. His room was tidier than usual, his bed made, his clothing neatly folded on his desk. His nightstand usually littered with plastic pill bottles and sleeping medicine had been dusted into the trash pale.

"Paisley, you're my best friend. I would never do anything to hurt you. I don't wanna fight with you. I love you, I'm sorry. I won't sell to Ray anymore either. Just tell me what to do to make it better." I didn't know what to say to him. I felt like such an idiot for yelling at him the way mom did at Chris. He grabbed my hand and put the knuckles to his lips. He inhaled deeply. "Please Paisley. Come on, I don't wanna fight with you."

"I'm sorry. I freaked out. I don't know what happened. I've had the weirdest day and last week I did get sick. I'm not lying to you. I mean I don't know what was wrong but I-"

"I punched a wall." He looked down at our hands.

"What? What are you talking about?"

"My hand. I got pissed and I punched a wall. That's what happened. I lied to you because I didn't want you to know, but I don't want to lie to you anymore. One of the kids at the Winter Welcoming Bonfire got caught drunk driving last month and he gave my name up to get out of it instead."

"Shit, well what's gonna happen to you? What does that mean?" My chest tightened.

"He doesn't have any proof because I sold it to him there that night. After that and Aggie having me arrested on Christmas, the cops are parked all the way up my ass now. At least she got me a lawyer." I couldn't believe Aggie had actually done something to help him.

"Ok, you don't need to just stop selling to Ray, you need to stop selling to everyone. Is that why you've been acting so weird?" I asked.

"Yeah, I guess. I just wanted to keep you out of it. I know you want to go to college now and that might not happen if you get pulled into it."

"I don't care about going to college anymore. Let's go to California like you said and we'll make it work," I threw my arms around his neck and pressed my lips into his. He pulled me in by the hips and hugged me quenchingly. I crawled into his lap and wrapped my legs around his torso. As he hummed into my mouth, I felt the same wave of warmth flood over me. He never stopped having an effect on me. He was always my favorite place. The idea of him not being *there* terrified me.

"Paisley." He pulled away. "You're going to college."

# 18

# No Getting Rid of Your Brain

66 The cafeteria smelled awful, like something dead had begun to rot. When I looked around to see where it was coming from, I saw a blue fog coming down from the vents. It's covering the ceiling in storm clouds. Thunder clapped through the announcement speakers and there was this scream and then crash. People started panicking, rushing through all the doors and then Giuls rammed into me and started pushing me and pulling me telling me that we had to go, but no sound came out. I saw everything she was screaming in yellow subtitles across the air. I kept trying to ask her what was happening, but then I realized I couldn't talk either and I started tearing at my throat and my skin started coming off with it. I screamed and then I woke up in my bed. I thought the dream was over, but then I heard these sirens coming from outside. There were ambulances and cop cars. I rushed outside and there was yellow tape around a body on the floor and the blue thunder clouds started to roll in around it. The same loud crash sound came in again and the body stood up and walked towards me. Everything was blurry and I couldn't see through the blue fog, but then it got closer. It was Ben. He had pieces of glass stuck in his face and his eyes were gone. They were just empty sockets and he said, "I'm sorry Paisley.""

"Did anything happen after that?" Dr. Yepez asked, looking up from their notepad. They had dark curly hair, honey colored skin and trimmed square nails.

"No, that was it. But I keep having the same dream. It's like the one my mom had when my dad died in a car crash."

I tucked my hands underneath my thighs to keep them from shaking. This was my second appointment. I hated the smell of their office. It smelled like stale crackers and glue. I agreed to go and give it a fair try, but I hated it.

"Well what do you think it means?" They asked me, staring down at my tucked hands. I felt like they were always analyzing me and asking me stupid questions. Obviously, the dream meant I was scared of losing Ben and my brain was recreating the accident that happened to my father. It didn't take a genius to figure that out.

"That I'm scared of what will happen to Ben because he's gotten into trouble," I said, calmy putting my hands back into my lap.

They looked back down at their notepad. "But what about the blue clouds? What about those? And losing your voice. Those seem to me like a manifestation of a pain that you might be working through."

"I guess so," I mumbled.

"Dream analysis isn't a science anyhow. You can learn a lot about yourself from them, but only of course if you're willing to really see them."

"Ok, but what about *what happened?* Is it connected?" I asked. Their office looked like the ones on TV, old leather, hard covered books lined on shelves, oak desk, a clock in my line of vision, black arms ticking towards the hour. I felt like exactly what I was - thirty minutes of their day that they had to get through. I could relate.

"Well it seems your panic attacks are connected to the loss of your aunt and your repressed grief." They spoke so coldly. I wish they wouldn't make it so obvious how many times they had told people what was wrong with them. It made me feel like a broken toy. "It's hard to say for certain, but both panic attacks occurred after instances when you were reminded of her death, when you felt close to her and once that feeling left, you had panic attacks and those panic attacks triggered depressive episodes which seem to physically impair you and according to your mother's description, leave you quite immobilized."

"If you knew all that already, then why did you want to hear about my dream? Why didn't we just talk about how to fix the panic attacks?" I asked angrily.

"I'm a therapist Paisley, not a psychiatrist. I'm here to give you the tools you need to work through your panic attacks and instances of depression. In order to do that, I need to gain a better understanding of how your mind works. And you do too. There's no getting rid of your brain, there's only getting better at understanding it."

---

"It was awful," I gushed to Will while we organized the yarn aisle. "They're like a robot. They just said I suffer from depressive episodes without even blinking. How do you say that to someone without some kind of empathy in your eyes? I swear sometimes their brown eyes look black. Like there's more pupil than normal."

At first, working at Lohanne's was supposed to be to save up for college, but lately I found myself taking every shift I possibly could. It was always menial tasks like color coordinating paper and putting yarn back in their proper baskets, but it felt good to be able to do something right. Plus, Will was there and I'm not sure how it happened, but he ended up being the only other person besides my family that I told about going to therapy. I meant to tell Ben, but he was so stressed and paranoid about everything that I didn't want him to have to worry about me too.

"So, it's depressive episodes?" He asked peeling a sku-sticker off of the organizer. "Yeah, I've heard of those before. My mom has them, but my dad calls them her temper tantrums."

"That's awful," I exclaimed. "But yeah, that's what they say, but they have seen me twice. How could they know after just two sessions?"

"True," Will said, smoothing out the new sku-sticker.

"Ok what is it?" I demanded. "I can tell you're not saying something."

"Nothing," he shook his head. It was so frustrating when he clammed up like that. The closer I got to Will, the more I could see what Giuls was always complaining about. He handed me two yellow rolls of yarn. "Ok, it's just that I think it's good you're seeing a therapist. It seems like your Aunt and your mom and Ben and everything in your life is all over the place. I don't know how you do it."

"What do you mean?" I asked, on the offense.

"You just don't have any stability," he said.

"Oh, ok so you're a therapist now too, huh? How lucky am I?"

"Hey, you asked," he laughed halfheartedly, leaning against my yarn basket. I pulled it out from under him. "My therapist says stability is the soil for good mental health. It's like this. When you learn a new language, it's really hard, right? It's confusing and you keep getting words all mixed up and the answer wrong, but eventually it gets easier because you figure out how the language works."

"Why don't you stop trying to teach me something and just tell me what you really want to say Will," I shot back at him.

"Damn, fine. You're making everything harder on yourself because you think it has to be this way for you. Like this is the way your life is supposed to be or some shit just because your brain is a little bit different than other people's. You keep tunneling yourself deeper into it, but you deserve to be happy Paisley," he drilled.

"Why does everyone keep saying that to me? Like I don't want to be happy or something. Why would I knowingly sabotage myself?" I said, annoyed, tossing the goldenrod hued rolls of yarn into my basket.

"Because that's what depression does to people Paisley. It makes your brain sick and it tricks you by saying twisted things and making it feel even more horrible things and if you don't try to understand it's language then you're going to end up just like Weston." He said sternly, his eyes watering and voice trembling.

"Will." I lightly placed my hands onto his. "I'm not going to end up like Weston, ok? I promise." Tears started to bead from his eyes. I held him in my arms, feeling his rib cage inflate. It felt strange to wrap myself around someone so tall and wide, like I didn't have the arm length to do it right. He suddenly pulled away from me, ripping his hands at the skin beneath his eyes.

"Just don't tell anyone please. No one knows, but me and my family. They would kill me if it got out," he pleaded with me, his red lips steaming.

"I won't say anything Will, I promise. I can finish the yarn if you wanna go home," I offered.

"No, that's the last thing I want to do right now," he scoffed and went back to work.

---

The revelation of Weston's suicide jolted me. A part of me believed Will didn't just let it slip, that he wanted me to know about what really happened to Weston. Maybe the secret was gnawing away at him or maybe he really was scared about what might happen to me. I felt so horrible for Will, having to lie about his only brother so he could keep up with his family's cover. It all made sense now, how he was always so quiet because he was afraid the truth might slip out. He probably only had a part-time job so he could be somewhere that he didn't have to hide.

*There's no getting rid of your brain, there's only getting better at understanding it.*

I didn't know what was wrong and it was stupid of me to push away the idea of therapy just because I didn't like what they were telling me. Of course, I disliked them- they were the one person telling me the truth. *They were still an asshole.*

The truth was that I knew something was wrong for a very long time and I kept pushing and pushing it back to the corners like overgrown cuticles. I had convinced myself that not only could I handle the pressure, I wouldn't place it onto the people I loved. The panic attacks and depressive episodes were my body's way of telling me that I couldn't handle it on my own.

*"Our bodies have physical reflexes to pain and most of the time, a detectable source of impact. Our brains have complex reactions to the world around us. The true cerebral toll of trauma reveals itself in curious ways."*

Will understood better than anyone else what sadness looked like in another person's eyes. Maybe I really did scare him and just like Ben, he could see something in me that I wasn't capable of seeing in myself.

Overwhelmed with the chaos and uncertainty of an organ that felt like a burden, that night I held my legs into my chest and thanked my body for being my shelter.

# 19

# Want Things for Yourself

Giuls lectured us on the rite of passage that is prom and the indie film moment we were entitled to as teenagers. She insisted we go, constantly reminding us each time how it may be the last real memory we would have of one another. Will always started scratching his ears every time she pressed on the topic.

"And Ben's birthday falls on prom. It's a dual celebration. We have to go!" She begged.

"You mean prom falls on my birthday," Ben corrected her. She rolled her eyes.

"Well I'm in," I said. Giuls beamed towards me and squealed. It was obviously important to her, so it was important to me.

"Alright then. Will you be my prom date?" Ben asked coyly.

"No, I'm already going with someone else. I'm going with Giuls," I said, eyeing Will. He looked up nervously towards me. "I'll go with Giuls and you can go with Will. I always imagined I would look good in a tuxedo."

"I know just the fit," Ben fluttered his eyelashes playfully.

I got down on one knee in front of Giuls and she burst into laughter, her cheeks burning with color. "Will you, Giulicia, do me the honor and be my date to Senior prom?"

"I thought you would never ask," she threw her arms around me, grabbed my face and crushed her lips into mine. She hopped into my lap and carried on with her plans about flowers and dresses and pregaming. All we had to do was show up and she would plan the rest. I thought back to that day on the bleachers, how she seemed so bland and detached. Now here she was, dazzling. I was so lucky to have her, a friend that seemingly spoke all of her thoughts out loud, like this ever-flowing stream that powered her mind. She vivaciously filled rooms with conversations and ideas. It was Giuls that brought us all together and set the spark. To connect at all with another person was impressive by my standards, but she had a talent, a magical way of connecting people. Giuls didn't let other people *see* her, she let other people know when she wanted to be seen. I imagined her standing in front of the Hollywood sign, larger than life, her hair blowing in the wind like an old movie poster, the kind you could hang on a bedroom wall.

At the end of lunch period, Ben's name sounded from the announcement speakers. You could hear the snap of necks in his direction. He gripped my hand tightly beneath the table. We all looked at one another in a panic, knowing what would happen next. "Guys, it's fine," Ben tried to calm us. "I'll see you after school?" He asked me. I nodded yes and he kissed my cheek. "Pais, don't worry. It's fine."

Ben Rosen, the neighborhood florist, walked through the silent crowd, his light steps forward setting off whispers behind him.

When he finally walked out of the room, their faces turned towards us with this filmy sheen, like a reflection from a TV. They were spectating, piecing together clues, sewing up timelines and theories. They all knew something deeply personal and intimate about us and we didn't have a choice in the matter. They knew about Ben's parents, about Will's brother, about Giuls' father, about my aunt. The Inconsolables were a spectacle, looking out from the inside of the screen. Our greatest losses were there on display, like blue clouds hovering above our heads.

\* \* \*

When I walked home from school that day, I saw Ben sitting on Hank's front steps. Hank died from a heart attack the night before and with no children or family of his own, he left everything to Ben. He was named the sole beneficiary in Hank's will. It was too much, but Ben couldn't refuse the burden. Another crack had rung through Ben that day and all of my strength couldn't keep it from widening. The butterfly effect was still in motion. The reverberation from his parent's car hitting that tree was still going off, constantly shaking the world beneath his feet. We sat for what felt like hours, silently.

Eventually he turned to me and said, "We used to talk about my dad." He sniffled and wiped his nose with his sleeves pulled over his fingers. "I'm really mad. I'm mad that I don't have anyone to tell me anything new about my dad anymore. It's like he's really gone now. I should be upset about Hank, but I'm mad at him instead. That's fucked up, isn't it?" He practically choked on his words.

"No, it's not. You're allowed to be angry. You're entitled to your emotions." I tried to reach for his hand, but he quickly ripped it away. "I'm sorry, I didn't mean to upset you more."

"It's all falling apart again...can you go Paisley?" He said turning away from me.

"Ben, I don't want to leave you-

"I want you to go," Ben said again. "Please go."

"But we can never leave each other, remember?" My eyes started to swell, but I wouldn't let myself cry and make things worse. His head fell down into his knees and he sobbed loudly into them, rocking back and forth. He was wounded and in pain. I wished I could take it from him to share between the four of our shoulders and arms. He wouldn't let me touch him. He cradled it there in his chest.

---

Giuls and I were at her house dying the bleached ends of her hair blue for prom. It wasn't for months, but we both decided the shade needed to be absolutely perfect. Prom fever was infectious, like this buzzing in your gut that made you wind up like a toy doll and every once in a while, we would just grab each other's hands and scream about things for no reason at all. The countdown was on and I was so grateful for something to be happy about without the omnipresent guilt. I had never been to a prom, but I always imagined speckles of light on the linoleum floor and cheap streamers and cardboard stars and tulle dresses and slow songs. Being around Giuls made me feel like the world was within reach and it was ok to stretch out your arms. *It's ok to want things for yourself.*

I finally got the hang of working with the annoying rubber gloves and lightly pressed the blue dye into the last scratchy strand of loose hair. Giuls read the final instructions on the back of the box aloud, "Let it sit in foil for forty minutes and rinse with warm water. Well that's a long time. I wish Ben still sold so he could give us free weed." I stared back at her in the mirror and rolled my eyes. "Sorry, sorry. I'm just saying, it would have been nice to smoke a little."

"You don't have any left at all?" I laughed, biting down on the plastic comb to free both my hands.

"I smoked it all!" She screamed to the ceiling.

"No!" I yelled, with her to the heavens. I wonder how many clouds we put up there. We were unapologetically as loud and obnoxious as we wanted to be. Why not take up the empty space? Why not smoke every last bit you can? Why leave anything left for later when you can have it all now? *It's ok to want things for yourself.* My phone started to vibrate on the counter. "Shit. Can you see if it's my mom?"

Giuls grabbed my phone and her eyes darted back and forth in a panic. "What is it Giuls?" I said dropping the comb. "Giuls, what happened? Read it!" I shouted, my blue stained hands in the air.

"Ben is breaking up with you. Over text." She put the phone down emphatically.

"What are you talking about? What does it say?" I sneered in disbelief.

"It says, I'm breaking up with you. I'm sorry that I'm doing it over text."

\*\*\*

"Paisley! Stop! You don't even have your permit. You can't drive!" Giuls screamed from behind me as I stormed towards her mother's car in the driveway. The tin foil still folded into her hair clattered around her cape blowing in the wind. With absolute confidence, I truly believed that I would learn to drive in the moment, like the protagonist in a heroic storybook in a moment of flight. I swung the car door open and slammed it behind me as Giuls banged on the window through muffled shouting. I put the key into the ignition and... well the car didn't start.

I rolled the window down and politely asked Giuls, "Would you please drive me to Ben's house?"

She threw her hands in the air and sighed as we switched spots. "What are you gonna do Paisley?" Giuls asked me with two hands on the steering wheel.

"I don't know, but he's clearly gone insane!" I yelled.

"Paisley, Hank was like his uncle. And he just *died*. Of course, he's going insane. What are you going to do? Tell him to get over it?" *Well, yes.*

"No, of course not! But I'm not going to let him just... just... fuck!" I said throwing my fist against the roof. The car rolled to a stop just down the block from Ben's house.

179

"Paisley. When Will broke up with me I was devastated, but your mom told me something that really put things into perspective for me. She said that when people leave, you have to let them go or you'll lose yourself trying to find them instead."

"Do you think Ben's really leaving?" I asked, desperately.

"I don't know, but he won't find his way back if you're gone too." She smiled softly at me, knowing the callous truth about the way people leave and the shape of their shadows as they walk away. She grabbed my hand and held it tightly in hers. "My mom is going to kill us for taking the car."

"I can't believe my mom gives such good advice. Where did she get that from?" I cry-laughed. Blue dye started to drip down Giuls' face and I burst into hysterics over how silly she looked and stupid I felt.

She spurted out giggling, shaking her head and yelling, "it's not funny! She's going to be pissed." We were both in tears, wheezing out in laughter. And we weren't even high. We sat there for three hours going back and forth, my core aching from not being able to stop laughing.

I remember how it started to drizzle, how the windows fogged up, how sorry I felt for myself, how funny it all was despite it. We talked about how none of it would matter twenty years down the line, not the essays or the boys or the hallways or the parties. With stars in her eyes, she rolled out her California dreams like a map, raving with fury about how she would overthrow the Hollywood regime and gatekeepers, smoke cigarettes in dingy jazz clubs on metallic boulevards, how she would be the next great artist manager who went down in history as "the woman with an eye for legends," like Philoctetes and Hercules. She was ready to give it all up, pack her life in a suitcase, build her empire from the records on her bedroom floor, and one day be there to see her legends walking out into a sea of stars. Inspired and beaming, she said that the great artists of the world were like constellations; painted in the sky, flickers of hope in the darkness, and a reminder that greatness was possible for anyone who remembered to look up.

Maybe it would be ok to want that for myself – my version of it.

# 20

# Casualties *

en was out of school all week again. I stared at his empty seat beside me in the cafeteria, dodging glances from students and completely at a loss for what to do with my hands. My thumbs twitched nervously at my palms and I bit at the skin on my fingertips. Rumors swirled that he was already in juvie serving time. People readied themselves to immortalize him as, "that one kid who went to jail in high school." Maybe he would have preferred it to, "that one kid whose parents died."

I couldn't wait to be at work amongst the crafts and baubles that you could rely on to put things back together, like sewing needles and zippers and super glue and buttons. Forever is an illusion for humans but inanimate objects without blood and feeling, like spindles of thread, fake flowers, spools of silk - those would last long after we were gone.

It was the last class of the day and I slipped comfortably into a memory still crisp. Ben and I staggered through Aggie's front door, face to face, ripping off our jackets like they do on TV and then *blam*, *whimper*. We had tripped over the little Pomeranian ball of fluff. The left side of my face smacked into the coffee table. I had to ice my eye all night so it wouldn't swell. Ben put a pot of water to boil to make us mac & cheese. I sat there with a bag of frozen broccoli stuck to my head and the caramel cotton ball of a dog rolled into my lap.

"I just got really weird deja vu," Ben snickered. "Like your body just turned into Aggie, I'm a little grossed out." He said shaking the goosebumps away.

"Hey!" I threw a crumpled napkin at him.

"No, no, like the much younger version," he said, fidgeting with the stove top.

"Gross. I don't even like boats." I pet at the dog's small nose. "So that could never be," I cooed at the dog.

"I didn't know you didn't like boats," he said.

"Yeah, the idea of being trapped on an object floating in the middle of a body of water. No one even knows how deep the ocean is. No, thank you."

"Hm, that's funny." He poured noodles into the boiling water.

"Why? Lots of people don't like boats."

"There's just a lot I still don't know about you. I wonder how long it will take to know you, I don't know, I guess better than anyone else." He shrugged. "It'll be nice when we can say that about each other."

"Yeah, it will be," I beamed back at him.

"You know when someone tells you something about themselves and you know, you take it in and without knowing, you've decided then and there whether you like that thing about them or not?"

"Like judging them?" I asked, laughing.

"Yeah, well I don't do that with you. When you tell me things about yourself, I just kinda write them down in this notebook in my head, like yup got it (he made a checkmark gesture with his hand)! I like everything about you, no matter what you tell me."

"That seems impossible, to like everything about a person," I said. "You can't think of a single thing you don't like about me?"

"I mean, don't get me wrong, you're insane," he rolled his eyes laughing, "but I'm here for it anyways. Whatever that says about me... eh, probably can't be good, but fuck it."

End scene. The metal bell clanged again. *Why does love take life's casualties and turn them into painful memories?*

---

The devil is merely a gatekeeper, we're the ones who put ourselves through hell. Chemical compositions are gluttons for chaos, twisting the quiet into the sound of being held down by the ocean. No sleep for the sad. No morning for the restless.

In the evenings, I *nightmared* of him dead and at dawn, I felt his fingers missing from the spaces between my ribs. I'm bad at missing people. All I can do is think and dream of him being *not there.*

*In the dream.* We stood around the boy with weak bones and shut green eyes in his open casket lined with silk. He was dressed in his prom tuxedo but covered in loose graveyard soil and blue roses with long dried stems.

"Just like that, in one massive blow. No pain. That's how my brother did it," Will said hitting the blunt. Aggie stood next to him in a Hawaiian shirt with sunscreen on her nose, sipping on a pina colada, and said, "He looked just like him. Drank like him too. I tried. I really did." Giuls reached for the blunt, her entire head covered in blue dye, dripping out of her ears and eyes, "From this day forward, there will always be something missing. I'm really gonna miss all the free weed." She coughed and coughed until Rex interrupted her, "Give me that," he inhaled deeply. "Such a tragical casualty."

"What is wrong with you people? He's gone. Can't you see he's gone and he's not coming back?" I cried and cried. I couldn't stop, the blue dye was everywhere, spewing from my orifices, like a poisoned fountain. "What's happening? I can't make it go away?"

Giuls passed the blunt to Will. He took a hit and said, "This is some good shit. What is it?"

"Blue Star Creeper," Giuls said, soaked in the blue dye.

They smoked and sipped till I was standing there in a puddle, my clothing drenched in the color. "What is wrong with you people?" I screamed again. "Can't you see he's gone? Please look at him!"

Ben's arm shot up from the coffin. Rex placed the blunt between his skelalton fingers. Camera pans down. He grins and says, "Don't be sad baby. It's only purgatory."

Mom laid out clean laundry on the kitchen table, her thick curls pulled into a hair tie that looked like it was about to snap. I didn't waste time. I wanted to know.

"What happened to you when Dad died?" I asked, startling her.

"Holy... Paisley. You scared the crap out of me. How long have you been standing there?"

\*\*\*

We sat together in the sunroom, the dust sparkling in the rays of light between us. She twiddled her thumbs around her coffee cup, tapping her nails against the ceramic. The sound of something unsaid. "Well where do we start?" She surrendered.

"I wanna know what it was like for you. Losing him," I said.

"Oh," she whimpered and swatted a tear away from her cheek.

She started by telling me about the day she was finally evicted from our old apartment and how she had to break in through a window to grab the last of her stuff. She left everything, but jewelry, Dad's toiletries, his pillowcase and his sweaters. "I was terrified of forgetting about the way he smelled. It was the one thing I still had that made him feel real, like he wasn't just gone. I took the shampoo and conditioner and soap and cologne and aftershave. I took what I could and packed it into a cardboard box. By that time, I had lost you guys and all I had left - all of it was in that cardboard box. I slept on a park bench that night. I could have gone to a friend's house, but I felt like I was supposed to be alone, that I somehow *deserved* to be alone. I couldn't figure out what other reason there would be." Her teeth bit into parched lips, tears rolling down uncontrollably.

"What did you do next?" I asked her, ice caught in my throat.

"I don't know. When I think back on it, all I can remember is what I was thinking about, what was happening inside of my head. It was like nothing else was real. All that mattered was thinking about him. I don't think of myself as addicted to drinking. I was addicted to drinking about him. When I was awake, I thought about how he was supposed to be there," she said, clenching her fists, "how insane it all was. I had all of these beautiful memories of him and from our life, but somehow all I could think of was this picture that was never taken. It would have been framed and hung in our living room and stuck between the pages of your yearbooks. It was a picture of the four of us as a family, standing in front of your high school on your graduation day. And you were wearing a graduation cap. You looked so cute and you had this goofy smile on your face. And I looked the way I did now, gray strands at my roots and wrinkles at the corners of my eyes. And he," she gasped for air and held her hand over her mouth.

"Mom, it's ok. We can stop," I held her other hand tightly in mine.

"No. You're right. You need to know. He would want us to be there for each other." She sniffled and took a deep breath. "He was older, his face thinned out from the years, his hair almost totally grey. He looked so handsome. That picture felt so real because he talked about it all the time. He loved you so much. I can still feel the pointed corners of that picture in my hands. It was so real to me."

I still have the nightmares. All the time. I still do. There's one nightmare of him wearing his cap and gown from our GED graduation, but he didn't have his eyeballs, just these dark, holes and he would say "Another eighty years of this baby." I couldn't stop seeing him dead. I saw him in doorways in the dark and he never walked in. It would fizzle in and out like radio waves. When it was quiet, I could breathe, I could let myself be tired, but then only a few seconds later, it would get loud again, and my body betrayed me. I needed him, to talk to him, to have him calm me down, to just *be* actually there. You know? I was so lost without him. It almost killed me, and I felt guilty for being alive every time I took a breath because I remembered that he couldn't. I couldn't sort out why I got to live. He would have been stronger than me, taken care of you guys. He would have been better, and I felt - I felt undeserving of life, of you and Kenny."

Just a few moments before, she hummed to herself over clean socks and linens and now, it was a totally different person unraveling before me. She lived with it. She spent her days with storm clouds in her head. Bewildered and teary eyed too, I asked her, "How did you do it? How did you live through it?"

"I just did. I remember having one good day and thinking, well this is never going to happen again," she laughed at herself. "But then the next day, it was easier and the day after was better than the last. By the end of the week, I had made it through an entire nine days without throwing up. And then I met Chris. He was sober back then, you know. And he paid for a lawyer so I could sue the truck driver's company and I was able to get back on my feet. I used half of it to go to a proper rehab, get out of debt and put down a deposit on an apartment. Just like that. One day, it got a little better. Better enough for me to crawl out."

Mom gave the other half of the money to Aunt Nadine and she used it to take care of us. I never knew it. I guess it's not a kid's business to know how food gets on the table, but I wish I had known it was my mother who had helped get it there. Maybe she would have still felt *there.*

She said that the hardest part were the days that inched closer, where there was more time without him, than there was with him. That was also the part that made it easier, whether she liked it or not.

---

That night I laid in bed, contemplating falling into another nightmare or digging myself deeper into one. I called Ben, hoping he wouldn't pick up so I could listen to his voicemail and hang up right before the beep. But he did, he always did.

He answered, "Paisley, is everything ok?"

"I miss you," I said. It just came right out.

"I miss you too," he whispered.

"Goodnight Ben."

"Goodnight Paisley."

I hung up the phone and went to my closet for one of Ben's hoodies. I slid it over a pillow and hugged it into my chest, breathing in his scent and spilled over myself. I wept for the boy who turned blue through and through in my bad dreams. I don't remember how long I cried or at what moment I finally fell asleep. But I know that it happened regardless. At some point, it got a little bit better.

# 21

# I Never Knew Who You Were

I played the scene again, tripping over the Pomeranian, staying there on the carpet laughing. It was like watching characters who were invented on paper. The movie was over, and I knew I would never get either of those people back. I could let her go if it meant she got to keep him company.

"Pai-Pai," Yvie said. "You daydreamin' again." I had a new nickname now.

"Oh right, sorry." I shook my head awake.

"What you always thinkin' about?" She asked me as we walked over to the registers. I shrugged my shoulders and she grinned. "You know I got bopped last night," she said stamping a price tag on a roll of bundled plaid, flannel.

I turned to gape at her. "Bopped? Yvie. Do you mean to tell me you... got laid?"

"Ya, it was a good boppin'. I was long overdue," she snickered.

"Oh my god, bopped? Who bopped you?" She cleared the counter and climbed onto it. She swung her knees like a little girl.

"Henry. We did it twice," she said holding up two fingers.

"No way," I gasped. "Henry as in Henry the butcher?" She nodded yes and patted the spot next to her on the counter. I climbed up too. "Do you like him?"

"I bop em' and leave em' baby," she sung. "What about you? You have boyfriend? That boy who works here... the tall, quiet one. What's his name?"

"Who Will?" I said, "No, no that's my ex-boyfriend's best friend." I said, frowning. She patted my back lightly.

"That's ok, you're young. You have fun and bop lots of boys and maybe girls and then one day when you're old like me, you come back and tell me. I bet you I'll still be here."

"I'm counting on it," I smiled. "Yvie, have you ever been in love?"

"Ya, that bastard left me for a younger woman with giant boppers he knocked up. Love is ugly ting." *Note to self, bop is a multifaceted term.* She raised her chin to the ceiling and closed her eyes. "It was someting though. We came to the country together even though my daddy tell me he was trouble. He was right." She began to laugh with her hands on her knees. "It was worth it. I wouldn't change a ting. We had so much fun."

"What did he look like?" I thought about how much Ben would love this story, the way we would have started using "bopped" in his vocabulary ironically and then all together, kept it in because he secretly liked it.

"Oo he was so hot," she dropped her head back down. "Big, big brown eyes. But he's dead now, but I know I gonna see him again and when I do, I'm gonna slap him in the face and tell him, I love you, you son of a bitch. I always hate his stupid mother." She slid off the counter, placing her orthopedic sneakers back on to the tile. She had fire.

"Yvie," I called after her. "What was his name?"

"Bhagyanandana, but I called him Bhagya."

"Did you ever fall in love again after Bhagya?" I asked, hopefully.

"Not like that," she smiled softly.

Will rolled by pushing a cart filled with decorative wind chimes. "What are you girls laughing about?"

"Nothing, just bopping around." I winked at Yvie.

---

The car dealership cast a stark dome of light above the town. As I walked home alone from work that night, I thought of myself in retrospect. It was as if the streetlights started to flicker to this whimsical tune in my head and the damp spring air made my clothing stick to my skin. The ends of my shoelaces pattered against the cement sidewalk and cars sped down Old Country Road like it was a highway. I was starting to recognize the sight, the smell, the taste of when everything was about to change. It felt like being the only one awake in a house filled with people, floating in a chlorine pool with the sun flickering in and out of your eyes, looking out the window of a bus driving through the rain on a quiet night, walking down a street and realizing there is no way back to some places. You can go back, but you can't get it back.

Miles away from a cemetery, but I could smell the cellophane bundled orchids. Sorrow filled my heart for all the change I watched come and go, never saying a proper goodbye to.

Change works like reaching the end of chapters when you thought there was more. Change works like the best song ever written and no one there to listen. Change is finding old polaroid photos, feeling your blood stop in its tracks and instead of crying because it's gone, you smile because you are infinitely grateful to have had it at all. It is impossible to measure and catch your breath. In less than a month, I was supposed to walk across a stage, collect a diploma and just know what to do next? The path would pave every which way and lead us in circles and towards pits and gaps we would fall through to get to other tracks. Somewhere along all those broken windows and closed doors, one day *we'll* be able to distinguish the pinnacle *moments* that truly mattered. But they'll be long gone before we're able to recognize them.

I racked my brain for the moments that would mean something one day, tearing rapidly through my mind, feeling the corners of the pages almost rip as I scoured through them. Like a home movie in my head, I saw the morning sun and the forest in his eyes, Giuls' laughter booming through the metal bleachers on New Year's Eve, Kenny cradling my head in his lap, mom and Chris having coffee at the kitchen table, Will hugging a bundle of sunflowers in his arms, Aunt Nadine sweetly humming to herself over the newspaper, Mrs. Skela's red hair shining like cherries in the summer, stars shooting before my eyes, turning the bend to reveal a lived-in home, the sound of sneakers running through tall grasses, the first sight of him in the summer air with sun-kissed skin, the same songs over and over again, swimming to the surface over and over again, parking lots, carpet angels, inhaling, watercolor skies, liquid courage, nicotine, denim jeans, music blaring from old car speakers, his hands, plastic flowers, Ben's Eagle, mac and cheese, bed sheets, lockers slamming, skylights. *Raging, thunderous, insatiable* hearts.

---

I put my key into the door. "Paisley." Of course, I knew it was him without looking. "I fucked up." He squinted at the dark sky above him. His breath fogged. Bags too heavy to carry were cast beneath his eyes. He looked so tired, so drained.

"What's wrong Ben?" I reached for his hand. He stepped back.

"I messed up, I messed everything up. You were right about everything and now we don't get to be with each other because I messed it up. I'm so stupid Paisley," he slurred, beating his fist into his head.

"It's ok Ben." I shoved my hands into my pockets not knowing what else to do with them but reach for him.

"It's not ok Paisley. I hurt you. That's not ok. Stop pretending like I'm the one who didn't fuck it up. I should have done better. I should be able to take care of you. And I can't. I love you so much. And now I have to go away and I fucked it all up."

"What do you mean go away?" I asked. My voice stayed calm; my limbs at bay.

"I'm going to rehab in Arizona," he declared.

"Rehab? What are you talking about?" I asked, confused.

"It's the only way I get out of doing time, if I go to rehab instead."

The way he couldn't look me in the eyes, the way his sentence rushed out like he had rehearsed it. He was lying. It hit me. Why he needed all that money. Why he was always, always high on this buzz even without ever seeing him take a pull. The cops, the secrets, the weird moods. Missing class all the time. That night of Ray's party and the way her mother yelled at him. He wasn't consoling her - he was calming her down. The night Ben got arrested and how obscurely he talked about it all. How he left out all the details about how he got the drugs and what he needed the money for.

"Ben, why do you have to go to rehab?"

"I told you Paisley. Because I'll do time if -

"Ben. Why do you have to go to rehab?" I asked him a second time earnestly. We both knew now, as if he had been lying to himself before that point too.

"I have to go to rehab because it's the only way I'll get out of doing time. I told you already Paisley. Ok, believe me," he read off a script. But his face burned with the steam from his flaring green eyes. About to burst, like a rattling pipe with the Rockaway ocean rushing in.

"Ben. Just tell me the truth. It's going to be ok. I promise," I said stepping closer to him, my hands now trembling uncontrollably.

"You're gonna hate me Pais. You're never gonna be able to forgive me." The tears dripped down his face, his voice devoid of emotion. For a moment, I saw the blue clouds hovering there above him.

Maybe I had known all along and accepted the only reality I was capable of handling. I was so scared of losing him the way I lost Aunt Nadine that I never considered all the different ways you could lose a person besides death.

"I'm never going to hate you. You can tell me anything. Why do you have to go to rehab Ben? Why, Ben?" I pleaded.

"Because I have to," he whimpered and ran into my arms. "I'm so sorry Paisley. I'm so sorry."

"It's OK Ben," I said holding him into my chest. "It's gonna be ok."

We stayed on the stoop that night till the moon shined through the morning sky. He told me everything, at least I think he did. I don't know if I'll ever get the entire truth, but I pieced together what I could. Ben was sick, he was addicted to Xanax and any other benzodiazepines he could get his hands on from different housewives around the suburbs he sold weed to. Including Ray's mom. The only person that knew the true extent of his addiction was Aggie. She thought I knew, that I did the same kinds of drugs too. *So, you two do everything together, huh?* Everything about Aggie ruining his life was really about her trying to save it. He said he was sick of lying to everyone, that he was going to tell Giuls and Will so that I didn't have to lie to them. I told him he didn't have to, but he insisted.

Yes, he had lied to me throughout our entire relationship and that gigantic lie made me question every moment we shared, but I couldn't bring myself to be angry with him there and then. He was always kind to everyone around him, so generous with his friends, so gentle with me. It didn't make him a bad person, *did it?* I

197

thought we were in love, but can you really be in love with someone who isn't even there? I was heartbroken for the love *I thought* I had, for him in pain, hollowed out and aching for the one thing that made him sicker. With eyes like poison ivy, the tallest boy on earth had his wooden stilts knocked out from beneath his feet and before my eyes. *I never knew who you were.*

---

On Monday morning, Giuls and I sat inside the girl's handicapped stall together at lunch. She shook her head in disbelief. "I just don't understand. How did he get away with it for so long? How long was it again?"

"He said almost two years," I answered.

"Basically, when his parents died?" She asked. I nodded yes.

Will wasn't angry with him, but I could see that he was hurt in the same way I was. There were so many blank spaces we would never be able to measure up to the truth. We didn't know how he kept it a secret for so long, why he hadn't told us, how we could have been so blind, how he got so good at lying. Will asked me the same question every time I saw him - "Anything?" And every time, I would shake my head. No signal. Static in the airwaves.

*** 

"This is the girl's bathroom perv," we heard a girl shout.

"Fuck off Maggie," Will grunted. "Giuls, Pais. You in here?"

We looked at one another surprised. "Yeah, we're in here!" Giuls hopped up and opened the door for him. Will walked in with his lunch. He sat himself down on the floor and began to eat.

"What are you doing Will?" Giuls laughed.

"I don't wanna eat lunch alone out there with everyone. They keep staring. It's freaking me out," he said with a mouth full of sandwich.

The three of us ate lunch in that handicapped stall everyday till the rest of the school year and did our best to stay out of trouble. We mostly talked about Ben, connecting the dots where we could, like he was a character in a mystery movie. When we weren't talking about Ben, we played the game and blew the smoke out the window. Out of habit I would turn to look where Ben was *supposed* to be and for the faintest moment, it was almost like he was. Then I remembered the only person to ever feel real to me might as well have been all in my head. The Benjamin Rosen I knew was just stacked stories and full of smoke.

*Change works like reaching the end of chapters*
*when you thought there was more.*

# 22

# Wonder Eyes

I t was the last sump party of our Senior year and nothing in the human world could have kept Giuls from dragging us to it. She said it wasn't about them, it was about us. She said, "we mattered." We believed her. It's important to believe someone when they tell you that you matter to them. *Please do it, they're probably right.*

The wolves descended carrying kegs, lighter fluid, tables, beach chairs, blankets, speakers, jerseys, bags of plastic cups, string lights, bottles and cases and pom poms and glow-sticks. Silhouettes appeared on the horizon where tall grasses met chrome skies. One by one, the bodies walked to the center, lit by the moon like a beacon. Howling, twigs snapping beneath our steps, the clank of stones dropping down around the fire-pit. The spaces between my fingers burned like paranesthesia, I felt light, dizzy, no arm around my shoulders to hold me down. I needed a drink more than I had ever needed one before which is a strange feeling for a seventeen-year-old. Or at least I thought it was at the time.

I could hardly remember the names of the people around me. Imposters. Had they been here this entire time? If they were all here, where the hell had I been? I took a chug from the bottle of discount whiskey Will passed to me, just like the morning after my first house party. Now here I was, unphased by the chemical taste of alcohol. When did that happen? When did alcohol start tasting good?

Rachel came walking down with Kelly, holding their bottles of liquor into their chests. Her blonde hair danced at the edges of her hips, her denim shorts cuffed around her cinnamon, silky skin. She was so beautiful, a teen dream scream queen baby. The finest Lolita I had ever seen. Tip your hats to the hips of a generation. I could barely stomach how perfect she looked on the outside. But then her glossed and plumped lips smiled at me, an "I loved him too," condolence. Our biology lived for boys who were built like him.

Will and Giuls walked by my side, all of our hoods over our heads. Our tribe was smaller, limping along. My fingers curled around the arms of a clock. *Let there be light in the cold cartilage between your bones.*

Music began to trickle into the airwaves, Hawaiian clouds hovered, laughter broke through. The fire tinted our skin rose gold and our eyes flickered like constellations, like points on a map you could follow back. You can trace your heart back as far as you can remember. *People never change, isn't a shame? Why isn't it great? We'll always be this way!*

Everyone stared deadpan, the way they did at lunch. Rudely, reflecting the TV guide menu. It's not that I cared what they thought of me, it's that - I cared what they thought of me *and* I hated myself for it. I tried to remind myself not to care about the things - I didn't care about. My wires were crossed. I couldn't tell my pleasantries from formalities. If it weren't for the alcohol, parties would suck. There, I said it.

"Shots, shots, shots!" The crowd cheered. Liquor poured into cups. Lighters went into the air. The music stopped. They were all waiting, ready to swallow it down. *Give the kids something they can feel. Give the kids something they can't throw up, let it stick to their insides like tar on lungs.* They're all waiting.

"To Senior Year!" Someone shouted.

"To the last Sump Sprint!" Another said.

"To the class of 2007! And the crowd cheered.

"To the Inconsolables," Giuls whispered to me and Will. We held our shots up together and said, "To the Inconsolables."

Someone threw lighter fluid on the bonfire and a flame shot into the air. A maddening sense of glee filled our souls, a freedom that is only granted on the thin line of "over" and "begin again." A little pleasant slice of purgatory. A lacuna. A gap. A thing that is missing but the space still resides.

Chris used to say, "there is a time and place to drink your sadness." Of course, I'm not sure it counts for someone who drinks all types of emotions. But for the moment, it fit. It poured through me like water, half whiskey, half woman. The music grew louder and the noise in my brain, that clammer that felt like lighting would against your skull, that choking that tasted like bleach would on your taste buds, that migraine that sounded like cities falling down would - it was gone. I stopped kicking around, fighting against it and let myself float.

We laid in the grass, staring up at the stars. My elbows to the ground and my knees crossed, so deliciously drunk, a fool who forgot herself for a moment to revel in love, to learn what it meant, to learn what the good shit really felt like. Precious youth, the indie-film in my head. This was the way my youth was supposed to look. It was my story. Be careful what you ask for kids. Bite your tongue. It might not be too late.

*Un joven corriendo, un joven muerto, ellos vienen por ti.*

This was it, the end of the story. It *could* all go away now. The best character in the book got killed off. Can it be over yet? What more is there to say when the person you love goes away? "Please, can this part just be over?" the reader said to themselves. "No, no it cannot because that is not how life works!" The writer shouted back at them.

When you think it's the end, it just means to listen closer, look harder into the folds, find something to latch onto. There's more, whether you like it or not and if you give up than you're the fool who copped out before you could be around to see the *best part.*

---

*The regurgitated false promise that life will simply one day get better is detrimental to the psyches of the youth's developing minds. Life does not get better, rather it's positive and negative velocity move constantly over and below the point in which we perceive it to be until the end of our perception as we know it.*

*If it did simply go up and up and up and faster and faster, then the speeding hedonic car would crash through the ceiling, fly airborne in the sapphire sky and crash into the evergreen moss grave, ending our vantage much sooner than calculations could imply. We needn't get fully better, only to improve our skills of dodging the flaming meteors speeding towards our lamp head orbit.*

*We needn't get fully better, but rather swim to the point in which we can float like a buoy in torrential rain over abysmal waters. There you are, in the black pupil of the storm. The ocean evaporates and suddenly you're shooting through like the meteor coming towards you in the mirror. You think you're falling out of the sky, but really, you're learning how to fly. I know it hurts, Wonder Eyes.*

---

Giuls and I were sprawled in the grass when Ray came and knelt down beside us. "Hey," she said nervously. We looked on suspiciously. "Look, I just wanted to say that I'm sorry. Ben said the pills were for you guys and I thought. Well I thought that you were -"

"A druggie weirdo," Giuls whipped out.

"Yeah," Ray shrugged shamefully. "And I thought that you were part of the reason my mom was on painkillers again. And that you knew... and I'm really sorry for what I said and how I acted towards you. To the both of you."

"We had no idea, we promise," Giuls said, apologetically.

"I know it doesn't fix anything but-"

Giuls cut her off, "Consider it fixed Ray. Happy Last Sump Sprint."

We toasted our plastic cups and smiled graciously at one another. In the moment, it really felt like we all actually meant it. At the end of the night though, Giuls would call it, "that fake ass apology."

"I'll see you guys around." Ray walked off to her Heathers. I wondered if they all knew about her mom too. Maybe we're all just really good at hiding and pretending everything is ok.

"You good?" I asked Giuls, throwing my arm over her shoulder.

She paused for a moment in thought and said, "Yeah, actually I am. If it weren't for Ben's freaky Pablo Escobar double life, you and I would have never become best friends."

"Pablo Escobar sold coke, not Xanax," Will said, plopping down beside us.

"Whatever. I'm sure Pablo liked Xanax too. Besides, if we can make it through this then we can pretty much make it through anything."

"I don't know. I've heard the real world is pretty tough." Will said, sipping on his beer. "But what harsher conditions are there than high school?"

"True," we said together, almost ceremoniously.

---

Triathletes ran a marathon through my skull, their spiked cleats stabbing into my eyelids. The ground shook as they trampled over the freshly cut grass until I saw red and then finally, I jolted awake.

"Whoa, you ok?" Chris said from the doorway.

"What?" I said grabbing my head, wincing in pain. "Yeah, what's going on?"

"I'm sorry I didn't mean to wake you, but you've got someone waiting for you on the stoop?"

"Tell him I'm coming," I said, scattering out of bed like a frayed cat.

"Coffee!" Kenny yelled from the kitchen.

"One sec!" I shouted back, speeding down the hallway. When I reached the front door, I knew with absolute undying faith that it was going to be Ben. We would run the last Sump Sprint together. Maybe he was hungover like last time, but it didn't matter because I would forgive him. We would choose each other, we would love each other more than we loved ourselves, we would do all the bad things love makes you do.

*I know it hurts, Wonder Eyes.*

... It was Rex waiting for me with a cardboard box in his arms, his onyx hair slicked back. He wore all black up to his sunglasses.

"Rex, what are you doing here? Is Ben ok?" I asked in a panic.

"Paisley. No, no everything is fine. He's ok. He wanted me to give you this though. It's your things, I think." He shrugged and handed the box to me.

"Oh," I didn't have the energy to hide my disappointment. "You freaked me out. It looks like you're coming back from a funeral."

"Well, black is the new black in New York City," he said lightheartedly. "No funeral for Ben though, just for my summer. I'm going to Arizona so I can be close to him. You know, just in case."

*beat*

"Too soon for jokes?" He toyed. *Yeah no, shit.*

"How is he?"

"He's going through medical detox at the hospital. Home wasn't going so well." It was so, so crude. I didn't expect him to just say it, to say the truth so plainly. I didn't know what recovery looked like and part of me really did believe Ben was just grounded in his room, listening to music, reading through pages. My eyes began to water. I had no idea what he was going through. The thought of Ben in pain, hooked up to a hospital bed. Rex swiped a sudden tear away from behind his glasses. "No please don't cry. I can't handle any more crying."

"I'm so sorry Rex," I said, cleaning off my face. "If there's anything I can do to help..."

Rex pulled me into an abrasive, firm hug, the box between us. And then he kissed me on both cheeks like they do in French films. He made crying look glamorous, no doubt a skill the Rosen's all inherited. "Take care of yourself Paisley."

What a horrible ending. I sat on the stoop with the cardboard box beside me. I knew it was just clothing and belongings left behind, but it felt like a hand was about to pop out. Then I thought how that might not have been the worst thing, for there to be a tangible piece of himself he could have given me to hold onto. If I could just have an arm, I could at least hold his hand. That would be enough to sleep with. I would be kept warm by science and my soul would be nourished by an arm that would scribble his spirit's ramblings. I would marry an arm if it were his and it were alive. I wish they could have turned his eyes into marbles, like a looking glass I could still see him through. Anything, anything at all. I would have taken it.

Maybe it's morbid to think of a severed limb and dismembered parts of a person, but I didn't care. Thinking of him as pieces, instead of a whole person that wasn't there anymore - for a single second it made me feel better the way it makes me feel better when Kenny plays with my hair and I pretend that it's Ben.

"Whatcha got there?" Chris said from behind me with mom and Kenny peering over his shoulders.

"A box from Ben," I said looking back out at Hank's house across the street. I guess it wasn't his anymore though. The dead can't own houses, only linger in them.

"You need any help with it? Like lighting it on fire?" Kenny added in. I heard mom swat at his arm. "Ow, ok. I'm just kidding."

The three of them sat beside me and my cardboard box. "Honey, we're really sorry about everything with Ben. We know how much he meant to you. And we just want you to know that we never thought for a single second you were on drugs too," mom said.

"Your mom's right. Even we didn't see it in Ben, and we've seen a lot of that in our lives. And we want you to know that we don't dislike Ben or think of him as a bad person or anything like that," Chris added in.

"Speak for yourself," Kenny interjected.

"Thank you for not thinking I was on drugs, I guess," I smirked.

Mom threw her arms around me as Chris handed me a cup of hot coffee.

# 23

# You're So Blurry *

A *memory.* "And I'm always thinking about what we even did before we started drinking and smoking and destroying ourselves? How did we ever get happy, you know? How do people get happy?"

"I think smoking and drinking, and I guess, drugs too, they give us a new idea of happiness," he said inching closer to me, curling his cold fingers into mine.

"I don't know, I don't think that's what they're supposed to do."

"That's what they do for me," he said.

"Me too," I frowned.

"Let's lay down," he comforted me, pressing his lips into the top of my head. I sat at the edge of the bed and watched him undress.

I had no second thoughts about Ben. I never thought about letting go, not even a little. And it hurt like hell to know he probably did. For me, it was sacred to see him slide out of his jeans.

He tossed me a pair of sweats. I went to zip the hoodie up and he pulled it back down. I left it that way. I leaned up on to the balls of my feet and kissed at his mouth while he dried my hair with a towel. I liked the sweater, deciding quietly I would try to sneak this one along with the other t-shirts and hoodies I took to sleep in. In turn, he started stealing my chapstick and felt tip pens. It was a fair trade, little tokens of one another. Sitting down at the corner of the bed, he slipped his socks on (because he couldn't sleep without them) and I stood over him, patting his hair dry now. He put his hands around my waist, kissed at the center of my stomach and lightly undid the drawstring at my hem.

"Why even give me the sweatpants then?" I asked, laughing.

"That is a very fair question," he exclaimed. We crawled into bed together and his thin arms wrapped around my torso. He curled his body into mine, dozing off together, his breath heavy and warm on my neck. I liked sleeping better that way. Right before I shut my eyes, I saw the empty pill bottles next to his bed, the ones that always multiplied, but he never touched.

*  *  *

I woke up again soaked in my own sweat and sick to my stomach. The cardboard box sat in the corner of my room, it's insides haunting my dreams like some kind of enchanted trunk. *How much of it was real? Was I just his coverup?* The more I remembered, the more it all seemed wrong and untrue. How high was he? For what parts?

What kills me the most is how much I don't remember. At least half (or maybe more) of the time we spent together was spent under the influence of whatever he gave us. We were always high. We were always drinking and washing nights away because that's what you're supposed to do when you're young, isn't it? The goal is to forget whatever it is that's eating you alive. The goal is to have fun, as much fun as you possibly can and when things blackened out of your memory, it was usually a telling sign that it was good they were gone. We always had *too* much. He was my favorite person to drink and smoke and dance with. He was my favorite person in the entire world. I wished I could remember every second, but so much of it was in flashes, sporadic moving images and those little home movies that never slow down long enough to look closely at. I wished I could playback all of our memories. *You're so blurry to me.*

I tiptoed out of the house in my pajamas and prepared myself to walk over to Ben's threw the sump. I knew he was gone, but I wanted to see the clues he left in plain sight for myself. The warm breeze danced through me as I jaunted over the crushed cans and plastic wrappers. I remembered my first sprint and the ice caps that melted off of my shoulders that night - how I felt like everything was going to be better. And then I remembered Ben, pretending to be at a complete loss for how he made it onto my stoop that morning, how I didn't make him talk about it. I should have, but would he have even told me the truth? The first and only time he ever really slipped up - and I let him get away with it. Is that why he wanted to be with me? Because I didn't hold him accountable.

My jaunt turned into a jog and before I knew it, I was racing through the field one last time. I pumped my arms at my sides like I had wings and ran as fast as my legs would allow.

*The Great Contender, The Great Rememberer*

I caught the taste in the air, that moment when everything is about to change. The flavor of memory. Gasoline, hints of clementine and saltwater.

And it happens like that. You get one sign, one i-don't-know-why-but feeling - that *you are supposed to be here.* For *all* of it. All of it. I just knew it in my bones. I didn't think about what I deserved and who would be around to see it. All I knew was that I was going to be ok. I was going to see the world and fly over mountains and write down stories about my adventures and dreams and the people I was lucky enough to have loved and been loved by. The air tasted like change. *Inhale.*

By the time, I made it to the other side, I was out of breath and practically limping through his yard, but I made it.

"Paisley?" Aggie said, slathered in baby oil from a lawn chair. "What the hell are you doing here?" She slipped off the side in a panic, holding herself up with one arm on the ground.

"Hey Aggie," I said, casually. "Ben has my final essay for school. I need to get it from his room or -

"Alright, alright. Go get it and make it quick before his brother gets back. I don't wanna hear any shit from him."

"Thank you, Aggie," I said running into the house through the back door. Aggie wasn't exactly sweet as sugar, but I felt awful for villainizing her all that time. I crawled up the stairs like a monkey with the last of my energy. When I made it to his door, an awful feeling in my stomach almost tipped me over.

The room was a complete disaster, his clothing thrown everywhere, his bedding hanging at the corners of the mattress, holes in his walls, his mirror shattered, the stench of cigarettes simmering and rising from the carpets. I began to dig through the rubble. I wanted to feel that hole in my chest, to stick my finger in the citrus wound, hook into the fleshy tunnel and come out the other side certain of what I had gone through.

"He already took all the drugs," Rex said, from behind me. I jumped, grabbing my chest.

"Rex, you scared the shit out of me!" I nearly shouted.

"What are you looking for?" He asked, lighting a cigarette.

"Um, ibuprofen," I blurted out.

"Do you have a headache?" He stepped into the room, skipping over the piles of clothing on the floor.

"Yeah. No, no I don't have a headache. Ben always had these bottles of ibuprofen around and they were always empty, but he never took any ibuprofen. And then, and then there would be more empty bottles. Always more empty bottles of ibuprofen all the time. I can't find them."

"The ibuprofen?" Rex asked again.

"Yes, Rex, the ibuprofen! I need to see what was inside the bottles of ibuprofen!" I shouted at him.

"Paisley," he said, coming towards me slowly. My fists felt locked to my sides. "You know what was inside of the bottles. It's not your fault. You know that, right? Ben is sick. That's not your fault."

"If I can just see what's inside them though. If I can just see what's inside, then I can figure everything else out. I'm so close. I know that sounds crazy, but I need to find the bottles," I pleaded with him.

He walked over to the bookshelf, pulled down the basket on top and gestured for me to look inside. There were hundreds and hundreds of ibuprofen capsules. He saved them all.

"But there's so many," I cried. "Does that mean Ben took that much? That he took as many that are in that basket?"

"This is the second one I found," he said tearing.

"I don't get it..." I whispered in shock. "But that's so many. I don't understand how I could have missed it. How does a person miss a hundred ibuprofen bottles and not think anything of it? How did I not see it?"

"It's not your fault Paisley," he said, carefully placing it back. "I knew he was different after mom and dad's car accident, but I didn't realize how he had gotten that way. He seemed so in control of everything and like he had a real handle on it. Eventually, I forgot what he was really like, which version I should be worried about."

"Rex, it's not your fault either." I tried to console him now.

"I know that, I do," he said, adjusting himself back into place. "But I'm going to take care of him this time. I promise."

\*\*\*

215

Sat in the center of my bedroom floor directly beneath the afternoon sun burning down from the *Serotonin Spotlight*, I opened the cardboard box. It was filled with my sweaters and chapstick and pens and notepads. There was a manilla envelope with the words scribbled on them, *you threw these away, but I thought they were really good and worth keeping.* He had saved and ironed out my half-finished poems and ramblings I had crumpled up and threw away that past winter. Three boxes of mac and cheese. My favorite black hoodie of his. A framed picture of the two of us on Valentine's Day. Withering blue roses. My favorite snack, a bag of chocolate covered pretzels. It wasn't a breakup box. It was a care package. At the very bottom there was a letter for me on yellowed loose-leaf paper.

*Dear Paisley,*

*I'm sitting in my bedroom right now trying to think of something to say that could make this even just a little bit better. But you're the one who has a way with words. I wish I could write you the most beautiful love letter in the world and tell you how sorry I am and for you to believe me. Do you remember the first time we met in front of Hank's house? You were so cool and pretty and I never thought you would like me. I'm still surprised every time you say you love me. I've been trying to remember the exact last time you said it to me, but I can't remember it. I can't remember so much of it. I hate myself for that. I hope you remember though and I hope you remember me as a better person than I was. I hear our memories can do that to the people we love. It's not your fault and there's nothing you could have done to change things. I promise. I know you probably hate me right now and never wanna talk to me again, but I need to remember the last time I said it to you. So, I love you.*

*- Ben*

I held the flimsy piece of paper in my hands. How could something that means so much exist as such a temporary, fragile piece of the

216

physical world? I thought of Aunt Nadine and all the drawers filled with old sweaters and boxes with papers and bins of useless report cards. A *thing* isn't just what we have left of someone though, it *is* a piece of them. I knew it then. I would know it forever.

All the memories were a faded recollection, but this love letter was a lasting image, a peephole into the past that was mine to forever look back on. It was real.

What now? What do you do when it's over and there's nothing pulling you into a new direction? Do you watch the gap, wait for the next train? Do you build a castle out of all the leftover broken pieces? *Come to think of it, ibuprofen bottles would make good building blocks.*

Struck with an idea, I called Giuls and Will, elated with the revelation. I wanted to form a plan. "I need your help with something," I declared.

"Paisley, prom is in two days. You've lost your mind if you think I'm missing my salon appointment with my hair like this. I can't look like Jack Frost in my prom pictures. And why aren't you at the cleaner picking up your stuff? I saw it there when I went to get mine this afternoon!"

"Oh shit, right. I'll get it soon. I really need your help though. We don't have that much time."

"I'm in," Will said. "I don't have anything to do."

"Giuls, come on. It's for Ben. I'll explain later," I urged her.

Giuls groaned and said, "what is it?"

"Meet me at Ben's in thirty minutes. I'll tell you then!" I squealed in excitement.

"Thirty minutes?" Giuls shouted angrily over the phone. I hung up and ran to grab my coat so I could head to Lohanne's before I met them.

"Hey, hey, where are you in a rush to?" Chris said peering out from the newspaper in his hands. I was still getting used to seeing him awake at normal hours, sitting around the house instead of walking around it in a cowboy hat with pots of water. He had been sober for a couple of months. Mom only told me and Kenny a few weeks back though, reminding us that nothing in life was certain, especially sobriety.

"Oh, I need to get to work to pick some stuff up. I'll see you later, sorry!" I said from behind me.

"Wait, you want a ride?" He asked. He must have been bored to death with all the free time.

"Actually, yeah that would be awesome."

---

Giuls, Rex, Will and I all commenced in Ben's bedroom. "Ok, now can you please tell us what we're doing here?" Giuls asked.

"Yes, we're going to make Ben a birthday present. We need to find all the empty ibuprofen bottles in his room."

"I'm not following," Will said.

"We couldn't find them before though," Rex said, discouraged.

"They have to be somewhere in this house. If he saved the actual capsules which served him no purpose, then he must have saved the actual bottles which he used to store, store -"

"The drugs," Giuls finished my sentence.

"Thank you," I said. "Let's start in here. Check the drawers and the closets, sweater pockets, everything."

We tore apart Ben's room looking for the ibuprofen bottles. In the closet, under the bed, in every pocket. Only four empty bottles turned up. There had to be more somewhere in a trap door or something. I pressed my ear against the wall as I knocked my knuckles against them to look for hollows. "Ok what are you doing now?" Giuls said laughing. "This isn't a murder mystery and Ben couldn't even figure out how to use a screwdriver the right way. Trust me I've seen him try to do it many times in woodshop."

"It doesn't make any sense. They have to be here," I said flustered.

Hesitantly, Will softly said, "I don't think they're in here Paisley. Maybe he used them all when he was selling, selling the –

"The drugs," Giuls reiterated. "Maybe we can get him balloons or like a Get Well Gift Basket?"

"No. It doesn't make any sense. And balloons? Why the hell would he like balloons? We're talking about Ben here, the guy that arranged a trip to outer space for us on Valentine's Day, the guy who gave us the name The Inconsolables in the first place. He basically invented *the* game. The game, guys! We can't let him sit in the hospital all alone on his birthday, letting him think that we hate him."

"Don't we kinda hate him a little bit for lying to us for a year and using us as his scapegoat?" Giuls said.

"Yes, a little bit. We're allowed to be angry. But not enough to make us forget about all the good things. They have to even out, right? We can't just let that be it. This is our *senior* year. We have to end it right... he's sick guys, not a bad person." I said, surrendered.

"You're right," Will said. "Let's keep looking. But they're not in here so let's think of something else. Rex? Any ideas what Ben would have done with them? Anything he said before he left?"

Rex's lips twitched back and forth as he puzzled over the moments before Ben went to the hospital. "Him and Aggie got into another fight, but they did that all the time. He did lock himself in his room for a bit. That could have been when he moved them all, but I don't see why he would."

Another revelation hit. "Wait. I know where they are! I know where they are!" I said jumping up and down excited.

"Well, where are they?" Rex said, buoyantly.

"They're in Aggie's closet. But we have to make sure she's the one who opens up the door. Come on, let's go get her!" I said running out of the room. They all followed behind me, rushing down to the yard to retrieve a leathering Aggie in the sun. It was like a new game, but one that Ben had no idea he had left behind for us.

"Aggie, Aggie! Ben stole something from your closet and used it to buy more drugs!" I yelled as she spilled off her lawn chair again in dismay. Rex looked at me in panic.

"What the hell are you guys doing here?" She sneered, trying to stand up. "And what are you talking about? What did that little shit do now?" She waddled into the house and we marched behind her, careful not to intrude on her tyranny. "What did he steal?" Aggie shouted at me.

"I don't know, but he said it was from your closet and it was the most expensive thing you owned. Check to see what it was," I insisted.

Aggie opened her closet door and hundreds of empty ibuprofen bottles spilled out from the closet like a wave. She screeched like a seagull. Ben had filled Aggie's closet to the brim just like he had when he was a kid. She stood silently, looking down at the bottles, and finally said, "It never ends with him. That son of a -

# 24

# Blue Roses *

We locked ourselves in Ben's bedroom, feeling at home the way we always had there. He wasn't with us and it left a lull in our assembly line, but it was as close to old times we would ever get again. It took us all night and a few pots of coffee, but by the morning, we stood proudly before a countless number of plastic ibuprofen bottles glued together to make a beautiful castle. "Palace-Painkiller," Will called it.

"It's beautiful," Rex said with a tear in his eye. "He's going to love it."

"Brilliant. Now how are we gonna get it to the hospital?" Giuls said, yawning and cranky.

---

We tied Castle Comatose (Rex called it) to the top of the truck's roof. "Do I wanna know?" Chris asked us, pulling his fake prescription glasses down to his nose.

"Nope," me and Giuls said in unison.

"Alright, you kids load up into the back. Let's get going."

Sat in the passenger seat, I looked back at the three of them with their eyes closed, resting their heads on one another's shoulders. The Spring sun illuminated all the little dust particles dancing in their tired breath. Soft guitar trickled out from the car radio as the engine hummed lightly over the road. The passing weeks that dragged on forever had finally caught up to us all. Little by little and now all together, we were different versions of ourselves, perhaps better for it, but of course we wouldn't know until we were far enough away to see the whole tapestry. Without knowing it, we drove away from the beautiful now, or *then.*

### The flavor of memory.

After a thorough investigation by the security guards (which none of us had thought to be worried about), we walked into Ben's hospital room all holding a corner of the castle.

"What are you guys doing here?" Ben said nervously, already welling up, alarmed at the sight of the ibuprofen tower.

"I'll come back to check up on you," The nurse said softly, walking out of the room.

"Are those-

"Yep, you can thank Sherlock Paisley over here for this one," Rex said, delicately folding his sunglasses at the collar of his shirt.

"Happy Birthday Ben," I said. He was hooked up to an IV drip and appeared so much thinner than the last time I had seen him. His curls fell into loose tendrils perfectly around his face. Of course, he would manage to have good hair, even bed ridden.

"You look like shit," Will laughed. "I got it guys. I'll put it down." As Will carefully placed the castle down on the floor, we all walked shyly towards the end of the hospital bed.

"I'm not contagious," he laughed, "just look like it."

"How do you feel?" Rex asked, worry in his gentle smile.

"Well, like shit honestly," he grinned. His eyes were paler, devoid of their emerald color. "I can't believe you guys came. I didn't think you would."

"Hey, I've been here like seven times already," Rex sassily remarked and placed his hand over Ben's. Their wrists both had matching hospital bracelets that said *Rosen.*

"Yeah, you don't count," Ben joked, gripping his hand into Rex's.

"I'm so sorry guys," Ben said sadly, the tears falling down his cheeks uncontrollably.

"Hey, no crying! Today is your birthday. We can do all that another time. We have one more surprise for you," Giuls said, running out of the room. Ben bore his eyes into mine, almost begging me to say something but I couldn't bring myself to it. I didn't want to ruin my new favorite memory of us all together. Even under fluorescent bulbs and in a hospital gown, he was my Ben, the one I still loved. He was my best friend.

Giuls walked in with a shiny birthday gift bag and placed it onto his lap. Ben struggled to sit up right, rummaging through the tissue paper. He pulled out a black denim jacket. "Turn it around," Will urged him. Across the back, in white painted letters, it read,

*The Inconsolables.* His eyes lit up and said, "No way. You guys really didn't have to do this."

"Yeah we know, but it's your birthday and no Inconsolable gets left behind," Giuls said proudly. The jacket was her idea. We all looked at one another, a glimmer of accomplishment in our eyes.

"And on your prom day too?" He poked fun at her.

"Yeah well maybe you were right about prom falling *on your birthday* after all." She shrugged her shoulders and sat on the corner of the bed.

"You know what this means Rex?" Ben said looking up at him. "This makes you an honorary Inconsolable."

"Oh, how absolutely honored I am," Rex scoffed, rolling his eyes. "I'd gladly hand in my chip if it means I never have to use another glue gun again."

We sat together in Ben's hospital room talking, the way we always had. It was like nothing had changed - except for the fact that we weren't high. Not a single one of us. My doubts and worries about never having known Ben – they faded away as he laughed at his own jokes and beamed light through every pore of his body. I held his hand, weakly pressing his thumbs into mine.

"Alright, I'm going to the cafeteria. Rex, Giuls, you wanna come?" Will asked them.

"Well obviously we're coming with you. We can take a hint," Rex said prancing out of the room. Giuls jokingly mimicked his words.

"I think you outdid me," Ben said. He made room for me on the motorized bed. I sat beside him, letting my head rest on his. "I'm really happy you came."

"Gym class," I said.

"Huh? What happened in gym class?" He asked.

"That was the last time I said it. On my tippy toes and then you kissed me on the forehead and ran into the locker room."

"Oh, that's right. I do remember that," he said smiling down at me. "Thank you for that."

"Your welcome," I said snuggling closer into him, aware of his body straining to stay up.

"Are we still gonna be friends forever?" He asked reaching his hand out to shake.

"And we'll never leave each other. We've cracked the code Benjamin," I said.

"Or made our own." The colors fled back into his eyes, but just for a moment. We shook on it and sealed the treaty of the youth with a kiss. The last one. He traced his finger lightly across my jaw. It tasted like a sad song, like crystal breaking.

"I love you Paisley," he said crying into my hair.

"I love you too Ben," I said back, letting the tears leak out.

"Well I love the both of you. Even though you're both a little bit insane," Giuls said, walking back into the room and jumping on the bed. Ben winced in pain. "Oh, sorry."

Will followed behind her and gently sat at the corner of the bed, doing his best not to tip it over. "Well aren't you gonna say it too?" Ben teased Will.

"I was getting to it. I love you. All of you," Will said, groaning.

"We're gonna miss you at prom Ben," Giuls frowned and took his hand into hers. "We promise we won't have any fun without you."

"Speak for yourself," I joked, nudging at his side. A knock came from the door.

The nurse stepped in with Rex. "We'll just need you to go in the waiting room for a bit, but you can come back right afterwards," she said.

"That's ok. They've gotta get ready for the best night of their high school careers," he said, sarcastically. Ben gripped my hand tighter, knowing it was goodbye for real this time.

"Listen, you. I'm going to prom looking like a troll doll because of you," Giuls said, throwing a piece of tissue paper at him. She gave him a kiss on the cheek and said, "Happy Birthday Ben."

"Yeah, Happy Birthday Ben," Will said, wrapping his arms around Ben tightly.

My turn came. I took a deep breath, pressed my lips into his and said with all the courage I could muster, my voice shaking, "Happy Birthday, Ben."

Wistfully, he smiled an, *I'm sorry*. Mine like an, *I forgive you*.

"I'll stay behind," Rex said, sitting from the windowsill. "You guys have fun tonight. Be careful, ok?"

It didn't matter where we were or how we got there. We were all meant to find each other in life exactly when we did, after the losses and tragedies and car crashes. Over the tumbling blue hills that had no foreseeable end to the average eye, were four kids sprawled across the living room carpet talking about their dreams and ideas of the world. Maybe it's silly to think that us all meeting was fate, but what else do you call those little threads intertwined that held the ground beneath us? We healed together and, in the process, our roots braided into strong limbs that held us up.

The Inconsolables taught me that it was possible to feel alive, even with a few pieces missing. And when you're really living, it's going to get messy and the stakes are going to run higher than the tallest wave you've ever seen, and the music will be so loud it feels like it's the blood running through your body and the laughter will roar out of your lungs like icebergs breaking apart and your heart is going to break so badly that those cracks will flood over and over again until the morning light comes and you remember which way to swim. To the surface.

---

We all lined up on the front lawn for photos. "I can't believe you guys coordinated without telling me," Giuls wined in her blue tulle princess dress.

"I forgot to pick up my dress," I said through my teeth, trying not to ruin the pictures being snapped. Instead, I swam in Ben's tuxedo, with a blue rose boutonniere pinned to the lapel.

"Personally, I think you all look sharp as hell," Chris said.

"It's a no, for me," Kenny said, like a judge on a talent show.

"I think it's cute," Mom said, snapping a picture of us.

"Me too," Giuls' mom agreed, snapping a picture on a disposable camera. "And you were worried about not having a date to prom. Now you've got two." She winked at Giuls.

"Whatever. We have to go before we're even more late than we already are," Giuls declared, trying to hurry us out of the manicured lawn when a taxi skid to a stop in front of the house. Rex ran out of the car and yelled, "Hold up people. It's a jailbreak. We need one more picture!" Ben swung the passenger side open and waved in his hospital gown.

"Ben!" We all shouted and ran to help him out of the car.

"I got it, I got it. I'm ok. Come on let's make this quick before they realize I'm not in the bathroom," he laughed, limping his way onto the grass.

"Parents, ready your cameras. We need to do this one more time!" Giuls shouted, swirling her finger in the air. We all huddled around him, holding him up.

"Should we ask?" Mom said.

"Nope," me and Giuls said together, again in ceremony.

It was the picture in our heads... just a little bit different than we imagined it. Giuls, with sea foam hair, Will in a ruffled powder sky tuxedo his parents despised, me swimming in cloth and Ben in a hospital gown. It would be wedged into the pages of a yearbook we paid too much money for. And one day we would dust it off and revel in the chapter of our lives when our lungs were strong enough to run through a stinky garbage filled sump to spite our broken hearts. *We owe it to ourselves to look back fondly.*

"I love you," I mouthed to mom.

"I love you too baby," she said back.

---

When I was a little girl, Aunt Nadine told us that if you could hold your breath all the way through the midtown tunnel then you would be granted one wish. I would take a big gasp of air just at the entrance, puffing my cheeks out and squeezing my nose shut. I remember the way my lungs felt dusty, the red brake lights streaming colors on the white tiles, seeing the light all the way down at the end. I never made it all the way through, not even once. But it wasn't about making it through, it was about the dizzy feeling you would get when you almost made it to the very end, when it all started to sparkle like diamonds. That's what prom looked like. The kaleidoscope of a tunnel you barely made it through alive.

Without a lick of liquor on our tongues, we twirled around the gymnasium, laughing and dancing with our Senior class of imposters. The disco ball shot prisms around the room with purple and pink paper streamers crumpled around our shiny shoes. Mrs. Skela waved from the sidelines, red like a heart. Punch bowls and cookies scattered on tables. Music blaring, vibrations coming through the linoleum floor. School banners hung from every corner. Shooting stars in eyes. Arms cheering in the air for what felt like the tenth goodbye of the day.

Then the dreaded slow song started to come through the speakers and the crowd began to disperse. Giuls grabbed my hand. "No Giuls, it's ok. You and Will should dance together."

"Are you kidding me? You look way hotter in that suit than he does," she winked at me and twirled me around.

"Happy Prom!" I beamed. "Is it everything you dreamed about?"

We rocked back and forth in a sea of spinning partners. I saw Ray from the corner of my eye, dancing blissfully in the arms of a boy who I hoped loved her the right way. "Well, I thought there would be a different person rocking me in their arms. So, I would say better actually. Yup, much better."

"I agree," I said, suddenly dipping her. She threw her head back in joy. It was almost time to go. I felt it ending, the moon about to fall, the garden gates creaking, the credits coming to a close.

---

Giuls, Will and I found ourselves back on the bleachers on the football field. We all agreed the same stadium lights seemed a bit brighter tonight. "This is much better," Will sighed in relief as he took a sip from a flask that he pulled from his jacket pocket.

It felt strange to be, *not sad* about something for once. Given the situation, I don't think there could have possibly been any better of an outcome. Was it enamoring and magical? Not really. But at least we were together.

"Have you had that the entire time?" Giuls asked, peeling off her white princess gloves.

"I was saving it for a special occasion. That special occasion being now," he said irritated, passing it to her.

"Oh god," she winced at the taste. "What is this?"

"My parents caught on to me taking their expensive stuff," he shrugged.

I took a sip, slinging it back as fast as I could. "Smart people. When do they move you into college?"

"A couple of weeks after graduation," he said, taking another sip.

"Me too," Giuls said sadly. "I can't believe it's over already. I feel like it all just really started, you know?"

"Hey, boo, boo! No sad faces or sad questions! The game never stops. You guys are both going to follow your dreams. This is a happy time," I declared. They both stared at me like an alien.

"I've finally rubbed off on you," Giuls grinned at me. Her puffy skirt sprawled out on the steps. "I'm just gonna miss you guys. What if everyone in California is like, I don't know, lame or has bad taste in music or something?"

"That's your job, to show them the light. What about you Will? Are you excited for Colombia?" I asked him, loosening my bowtie. Turns out dresses were nearly just as uncomfortable as suits.

"Honestly, with everything happening, I haven't thought about it. I'm gonna miss Lohanne's though. And you both. Why does it feel like the last couple of weeks happened in fast forward?" He asked.

"I know. It's total bullshit that our youth," Giuls said, holding up finger quotes, "is ending and we just figured out what was really happening. I don't wanna be an adult. I wanna sit on the floor, smoke weed, eat whatever I want and stay here with you forever," Giuls pouted, scratching at her dress. "My mom keeps telling me my body is about to change. It's so annoying."

"I'm gonna miss you too," I said.

"Why does it feel like it's time to go home? And it's only like ten o'clock?" Giuls exclaimed.

"I don't know. I have this weird feeling in my stomach too, like it's all ending," I admitted.

"It feels like this part is too short," Will said.

# 25

# Off the Record *

The July heat was unbearable, too thick to breathe through. Without really any reason to be outside, I mostly stayed in my room writing and shivering in the air conditioning. Still, miraculously I found that even my eyebrows sweat. It was my second summer in the suburbs, and I was restless, waiting on the next train, treading water in chlorine pools. I had been waitlisted and that had a very literal interpretation on my nowness. Waiting. I still hadn't gotten into a single college.

Twenty-six days since graduation. Sixty-two days till the end of summer. Eleven days of listening to the same record and losing track of how many times I flipped it from side to side. Innumerable days waiting for letters from Ben at rehab halfway across the country that never came, on calls from Giuls and Will to tell me about their new lives and what their dorms were like, on Kenny to come home from his summer job, and thoughts on how long I could lay awake in bed before I needed to use the bathroom. It was anticlimactic and though the flowers were brighter and the sunset cut neon stripes into the sky, I was going crazy, bored out of my mind. I even called Mrs. Skela once but her voicemail had said she was backpacking across South America.

On the weekends, I hung out with Mom. Chris left again. I couldn't count how many days it had been since he left. One day I just noticed I hadn't seen him in a while and mom said, "he left." That was it. She didn't seem sad about it. She didn't cry about it this time around. Her hair neither rose nor flattened. Kenny said he would be back. Mom agreed. I had my doubts.

We watched every Tim Burton movie ever made and when we made it through them all, we decided to watch them again. I picked up as many shifts from Lohanne's as I could to fill my time. Nothing was immediately wrong, but I still felt the grey fog roll into my head each morning. It loomed like a familiar season but seemed to come and go like summer rain.

I was fine though, or at least I should have been. I had made it through one of the toughest years of my life and a part of me felt indestructible, but the side of me I clearly had no control over dwelled on the dense clouds that grew heavier and heavier each day. I was so out of it at work one day that I stapled my finger. That's not even the worst part. The worst part was that I didn't realize till Yvie came over and gasped, "Holy cow, there a staple in your finger Pai Pai!"

The last few weeks of high school flew by in a flash. Graduation hats in the air, signing yearbooks, cleaning out lockers, the last bell ringing, walking down the empty hallway together, stuffed trunks, teary goodbyes, packing up Giuls and Will's rooms into cardboard boxes, waving from car windows. But I never got to say goodbye to Ben (again). None of us did. He just left.

When we took our prom picture, I had imagined myself grey and old with wrinkly fingers opening the senior yearbook and looking back on it. But I did it every day and its sharp corners pricked me in the same place every time. I missed the feeling of heaven when he was near. I couldn't help but feel that being without him meant I had been kicked out of the angel's club.

I was lying in bed, deciding whether to go pee or just go back to sleep when a knock came from my bedroom door. "It's mommy. You up?"

"Yeah," I said back, still lying flat, rolled into my comforters.

"You look cozy," she smiled. "You've been sleeping a lot lately. Everything ok?"

"Yeah I'm fine, just tired," I half-smiled.

"I'm going to the mall today to shop for a birthday present for your brother. Do you wanna come?" She asked.

"Sure, that sounds fun," I lied, already thinking of the dreadfully volcanic three and a half minutes that it took for the hot car to cool down and the way I would burn my fingertips on the seatbelt that was gaining it's evil power from the sun at that very moment. I slipped on denim shorts and went to reach for a white t-shirt, but then I chose the red one. I told myself aloud, "I'm going to wear red so that I don't feel blue."

---

The mall always smelled like stale ice cream cones, but it was nice to be out of the house for once instead of deliberating between bodily functions and menial tasks. Of course, we went to seven stores for mom and one for Kenny.

I browsed through a rack of red clothing when mom pinched my side. "Ow, what is it?"

"Do you see that cute boy over there?" She whispered.

"Mom, he's way too young for you," I said sternly.

"No, not for me. For you. He's been eying you. Don't look now but..." I went to look, but she pulled my arm back. "No, I said, don't look now Paisley."

"Well how am I gonna see him if I can't look at him?" I said, annoyed.

"Slowly. Act casual. Ok, now," she said. My head flipped around and back so fast that I barely got a good look at him.

"Oh, I think he's cute?" I whispered back.

"I know I told you. But I think you scared him off with your sad robot girl, neck flip thing you just did. What the heck was that?" Mom said, rolling her eyes and walking off.

*　*　*

"When do you think you'll start dating again, huh? Or do you plan to see how long it takes for Ben to come back from rehab?" Mom said, taking a bite of her ice cream. *Ok, harsh.*

"No," I shot at her. "I'm just not interested in dating right now."

"Well why not? You seem pretty lonely to me." Her hair peaked in curiosity. How did it always move so intently? It was really quite incredible actually. "You have to at least try."

"I'm not lonely. I'm just getting ready for college and resting my mind," I pulled out of thin air.

"Right and what happens if there is no college and you have to wait another year?" She posed.

"I don't know, but I don't think getting a new boyfriend is going to solve that problem Mom," I sneered, stabbing my ice cream with my plastic spoon so hard that it snapped.

"Ok point taken. No new boyfriends," Mom giggled, looking down at my dismembered spoon.

---

Summer is this strange linear time of life where it doesn't matter what day it is. Even when the sun goes down, it still remains the same hour. It is a constant inescapable delicious warmth and I was frustrated by nature's way of forcing me to feel it. Summer is the song that got left off the record. I got left behind. I recognized the same feelings of abandonment stir in my gut and I swore to swim to the surface. I would not go under, not like this. At least that's what I told Dr. Yepez. They grew on me after all.

Mom was right about me being lonely, but not about how to fix it. I figured there were bound to be times in life, no matter what you do, that the world will leave you on your own. If I was ever going to grow, I needed to learn how to be alone again. I needed to learn what it meant to choose myself. In the process of doing so, I hoped the rest would fall into place. In fact, I was banking on it. The next morning, I woke up and took the bus to the admissions offices of Nassau Courts Community College.

\* \* \*

"Excuse me mam," I said through the plastic divider. She spun around with a look of disgust on her face.

"I'll be with you in a moment," she sneered. "You can take a seat over there and wait for me to ring the bell," she said, pulling down the curtain.

"Got it," I said, seating myself down in yet another scratchy tweed chair. I thought back to Mrs. Skela and how her door was always open.

"Paisley?" I knew immediately it was Ray's voice that came from behind me.

"Ray, what are you doing here?" I asked, jumping up.

"I'm taking a couple of courses before school starts. What about you?"

"Um, yeah same. Kinda. Yeah, same deal kinda," I rushed through my words nervously.

"Oh cool. Yeah, everyone basically left already. It's kinda a ghost town around here lately... Have you um, heard from Ben?" She asked, timidly.

"No," I frowned. "What about you?"

"Oh no, I haven't talked to him for a long time...I think about everything a lot though," she said "Kinda hard not to when you realize your mom only liked your boyfriend because she was getting drugs from him. It's been pretty weird at home."

"Shit," I said, shaking my head. "That must be really weird."

"It is so fucking weird. How do you even deal with that? I'm not sure what kinda long term trauma I'm in for. It is just yeah, *really fucking weird.*"

The bell dinged. Thank *fucking god.* "Oh, that's for me. I'll see you later?" I said unsure.

"Yeah we should go get coffee on campus or something since you're gonna be here now," she offered.

"Yeah, cool. Let's do it. Cool," I said, all gummy and embarrassing. I don't know why but she made me so nervous. I couldn't tell whether she was going to kick me in the face or tell me she wanted to be best friends.

The bell dinged again, and the woman shouted, "Miss Ciel, I said wait for the bell. Do you not hear the bell?"

---

I used my savings from Lohanne's to enroll myself in a summer creative writing course and I loved it from the moment I sat in the chair. It felt so good to have planted *myself* somewhere. And they had air conditioning. And I didn't even need to ask to go to the bathroom. I could just go whenever I needed! I loved college! Well, I loved the one class in a college building. I also learned that you don't necessarily need to go to college to be a writer and my professor urged me to continue my pursuits despite making it past the waitlist or not. He said my writing was "sporadic" and that it wasn't always clear what I was trying to say, but that it was a good tag I could develop as an author. He said I reminded him of the

Beatniks. I knew them from the books Ben read. At the end of class, we would sit in a circle and discuss one another's work and talk in length about the ideas we cared about. It was just like the game, but not as funny. I couldn't help but wonder how much better the conversation would flow if we were all just a bit high. *Just a little bit.*

In the most interesting turn of fate, Ray and I became coffee campus buddies. It turned out, she wanted to be an English teacher and we were enrolled in the same creative writing course. We would read through one another's stories and talk about the authors we were learning in class. Sometimes, she went on tangents about her groups of girlfriends and how "over them" she was. They were mildly entertaining. When I was on campus, I could see this new corner unfold -

"Paisley, hey Paisley," Ray said, waving her hand.

"Oh sorry, I zoned out," I said shaking my head awake.

"So, do you wanna go?" She asked me. I stared blankly again. "To the party? Tonight?"

"Oh, um I don't know. Would that be weird if we went together?" I asked her, hoping she would agree with me.

"No, it's an all-years party. Most of the Seniors are gone anyways," she explained.

"Ok, yeah," I finally agreed. I thought maybe it would be good for me to go to at least one party. Afterall it was summer. And I didn't have any other friends. *Obviously, as usual.*

"Hey Kenny," I said, in the doorway of his room.

"What's up?" He asked, suspicious already.

I peered my head through and asked, "would you wanna come to a party with me tonight?"

"The one at Tucker Trigger's house? Why would you wanna go there?" He asked, like he was grossed out.

"Well Ray invited me and I kinda said yes because I was scared to tell her no," I said truthfully.

"Ray? As in Ben's ex-girlfriend, Ray?" He asked. I nodded a yes. "Ok. Weird. That guy's an asshole though. You sure you wanna go to that? His parties always suck too."

"Maybe, let's just go for a little bit and see how it is?"

*\*\**

"Ok, we can go!" I said to Kenny as we walked through the door. Suddenly, I remembered how much I hated high school.

"I was hoping you would say that," he sighed. "Let's get out of here before-

"Ah! Paisley! You're here!" Ray squealed and hugged me, shaking me up and down. "Oh my god, I can't believe you came. I am so happy you are here. Oh, Kenny you came too! Let's go get a drink!" She slurred her words. Ray was sweet and she was trying (for some odd reason) to be friends. Maybe we both needed one.

After thirty minutes, I decided I gave it my best try and it was time to go. Also, Ray had gone off to the bathroom with one of her friends and it was the perfect time to make a run for it. "Ok, let's go. Quick before she comes back!" I said to Kenny over the music.

We were nearly out the door when someone pulled my arm back. It was Tucker Trigger. "Hey Ciel, where you going so early?" He said, with a plastered smile, his pupils dark.

"I'm feeling a little sick actually. We're gonna head out, but thanks for having us," I said, turning away, but he tugged my arm harder.

"Ow, what's your problem?" I said, defensively. Kenny stepped in front of me.

"Sorry, sorry," he said with his hands up. "I just need some, you know," he lowered his voice and leaned in. "I'm looking to buy. You selling - anything?"

"No, of course not," I shot at him.

"But your Ben's girlfriend, aren't you? Can't you, you know find some? I'll pay extra," he said frantically. A bead of sweat dropped down from his hairline. *Who did they all think I was?*

"She doesn't have any Trigger," Kenny yelled at him.

"Ok, ok, keep it down. I get it. But if you uh, you know do happen to come across any. You know where I am," he squirmed.

"She gets it. Let's go Paisley," Kenny said, throwing his arm over me.

We walked home from the party, trying to laugh it off, but Kenny could tell that Tucker really got to me. I didn't feel like adding another bad memory to the reruns. "You sure you don't wanna talk about it?" Kenny asked softly.

"Actually, I wanna say one thing out loud and then I don't wanna talk about it anymore. I never wanna ever talk about it again because I hate that this keeps *fucking happening.* I just realized that Tucker Trigger was one of the kids at the Winter Welcoming Bonfire and it really pisses me off. There are all these ... these *things* that I just didn't know and now everything is clicking seven months too late. And lucky him, he's not around to have to explain it or to even be mad at. He just got to leave and *I'm the one* still here - having to deal with everything being completely different. And it hurts. It hurts to think of him and it pisses me off. I'm pissed off!" I fumed through my ears and finally took a deep breath and said, "I'm pissed off."

"That sucks," he quipped.

"I know!" I shouted into the night. "I know!"

*Summer is the song that got left off the record.* *

---

* 'I can still feel your skin (Chapter 25)' did not make it on to the 2020 version of the pressed vinyl record, but it will be released digitally in 2021.

There were many songs written for this project, which I love dearly, but unfortunately could not be added. I sincerely hope they make it out of the bunker.

# 26

# Outro *

The next morning, Mom, Kenny and I all sat around the kitchen table, sipping coffee, peeling pieces of bread from the center when the phone rang. "I'll get it," I said, lax.

"Hello?" I said with bread stuffed into the corner of my mouth.

"Paisley?" A woman shouted through static from the other end.

"Mrs. Skela? Is that you?" I asked her.

"Yes! Oh, it's so nice to hear your voice. Really any voice. I've been meditating in the jungle for eleven days now and let me tell you, I am never doing that again. But listen I can't talk too long, but I have to tell you something!"

"Ok, yeah. Ok, I'm ready," I said, leaning against the wall smiling at the familiar sound of her speeding words.

"I was checking my voicemails just now and well, you're in! Queens college accepted your application! You did it!"

"Wait what? I'm in?" I screamed. Mom and Kenny scurried over to the phone.

"Yes!" She shrilled. "And there's more. I couldn't tell you until you were accepted somewhere, but tuition is all taken care of!"

"Wait what do you mean? Like I don't have to pay? Like a scholarship?"

"No, apparently it is being paid for by the Rosen family. Student loans are not a pretty thing though, so this is a good thing. Listen, I have to go, but congratulations. You are officially a college student. You start in September!" The line went dead.

"Um..." I said, shocked.

"HOLY SHIT, YOU'RE GOING TO COLLEGE!" Mom screamed.

"I'M GOING TO COLLEGE!" I shouted in *sweet fucking triumph.*

---

The word "better" had become the bane of my existential, one-eighth life, suburban crisis. I want so badly to believe it, but maybe it doesn't get better. Better, as in, improved from its previous state. Better as in fixed. Better as in easier. Better as in new. No, it doesn't. It can't. Knee deep, staring at the letters in my head, it felt impossible.

Taste in music, scabbed knees, your balance on a bike; those can get better. I suppose you can get better at losing people, but them being gone - that doesn't get better. Does it? That is just what *is* and remains in their perennial absence. There is no grand resolve, but there is resilience and the nature of relativity and what comes next. There is a will to build on top of what was, there is a place to begin again.

The state of loss and its permanent wax seal on lives cannot be undone. That is what is so hard, isn't it? Knowing there are hollows that cannot be filled by the ground that once was. Some bones never heal right.

There are buildings that can be renovated, knocked down and rebuilt, but it doesn't erase someone from the walls inside of your mind. It doesn't lose the way the light spilled over the floors and the way it crawled into the birthmarks on skin and puddled irises in the morning. Or the sound of sneakers skidding across echoing halls. It happened, it was breathing, it was once the brightest sun in the sky, the tallest and most beautiful feat of architecture that ever was constructed on the planet that spun each day for *just us*. And when I think of it, gone like land washed away from storms, I remember it in shades of rose and I whisper into the ears swarming with static, "show it like it really happened, remember it right, *not better.* "

---

"Paisley, Paisley, wake up," Kenny shook me awake.

"Kenny? What happened?"

"Ben is on the phone downstairs, go get it!" Kenny hurried me, knowing how important it was to me that he had called.

"Oh shit, shit, shit." I ripped the covers off and stormed down the hall, dodging the me(n)tal pendulums.

"Ben, you there?" I said nervously.

"Paisley," he said softly. The line stayed quiet for a moment. "Paisley?"

My body melted right back. "Yeah, yeah. I'm here. Are you ok?" I asked.

"Yeah, I've been good," he lied. "I'm sorry, I know I haven't called. I was going to. It's been... it's been weird."

"It's ok, Ben," I said with the first tear dropping down to my chin. It came so quickly, it felt reflexive.

"You don't have to say that. It's not ok and I know that. I miss you so much Paisley. I wish I was there. I know I shouldn't call and this is gonna be the last time, but I wanted to tell you how much I miss you and how I loved you even though I didn't do it right, but I did and I -" his voice cracked. "And that I am so sorry. I am so sorry Paisley," he whimpered softly into the line.

"It's ok Ben, it's ok. I miss you so much," I cried, too. "Why does it have to be the last time? You can call me, and we can talk, we can just be friends, you know? Like we said?" I pleaded with him. I'd do it all again, build him up just to watch me fall over myself. Over and over again.

*I wanted to take your pain away, but I learned that's' not something you can do for anyone but yourself the hard way.*

"Yeah, friends," his voice shook again. "I'm not really allowed to call people. This is kinda, well my friend snuck a cellphone in ... Paisley, you're going to be so great next year at college. I know you're gonna be great."

"Oh, I can't believe I almost forgot. Ben, did you pay for my tuition to college? That's too much. I can't accept that," I declared.

"It wasn't me. It was Aggie. Shit, I have to go."

*Just like that, you were gone...*

---

I knocked on Aggie's door tirelessly until she finally opened it. "You don't go away, do you? What is it, Paisley?" She huffed, pulling her bathing suit wrap tighter around her.

"Aggie... why are you paying for my tuition?" I asked, perplexed. She stared at me for a moment like she had no idea what I was talking about.

"Oh, right. Well congratulations," she said, going to shut the door. I shoved my arm through to keep it open.

"Wait, I can't accept it."

"Yes, you can. I didn't do it for Ben, you understand me? I did it for you. I invested in you," she spoke, like it was painful for her to say words with even a hint of kindness laced into them.

"But you don't even like me. You don't even really like Ben."

"Hey, listen for the record, I love Ben. I might not be the best at showing it, but he was the one who chose to keep hurting himself. I had to do what I had to do - to protect myself from the pain of losing another Ben Rosen. I know he led you to believe otherwise, but there was a time I tried to save him. And I can't help him anymore, but I can help you. I was just like you, drunk parents, druggie boyfriend. I was all dough eyed and dumb, but I could have been someone. Instead, I lost myself in someone else with no future. Go to school Paisley, get out of this town and when you feel like giving up, you keep going, ok? Then we're even."

"Ok," I said plainly. I couldn't believe the words coming out of Aggie's mouth.

"Good, now don't come back here again."

The door slammed in my face.

*outro*

# BUILDING YOU UP

ALEXANDRA ALLER

## ACKNOWLEDGEMENTS

It has always been important to me to write the kind of book the younger version of myself needed. When setting out to write a coming-of-age story, I never thought, as an adult, I would need it just as much. In short, the story that unraveled became the path for processing formative years of my youth where I felt dejected and broken. Unknowingly, I harbored those feelings in me until they came spilling out.

So, here is that mess, those missing pieces - that I have tried desperately to turn into something beautiful. My two hopes for this project are firstly, that this is the first step to a blossoming, full life of continuing to discover the beauty in loss through art - and second, to give others a safe place to find theirs.

To whom this book is dedicated to - my siblings - please know that you are spectacular, capable of spectacular feats. Life in all its finite, is worth reaching for while you have the chance. To my family, I am grateful for you in this life, the last and the next.

Chiara Gerek, you exemplify possibility. Zoe´ Kraft, your unwavering confidence in me is bewildering and I am endlessly thankful to you. Mason Maggio, it is my personal belief that the same qualities that contribute to your musical ingenuity are derivative of your incredible human nature.

Thank you from the depth of my being to everyone who has supported my art, encouraged me to keep going or simply listened to me talk through tangled ideas. Create not within your means, but from your means.

ALEXANDRA ALLER